A Secret Room . . . A Secret Past . . . A Secret Murder

"Whew! That was hard work," said Thomas, sinking breathlessly into a chair. There was a large square hole in the wall now.

"Aren't you going to look inside, Mr. Harding?" asked the builder's boy. He could hardly stand still with excitement.

"Give him time to get his breath back, lad," commanded Charlie Ford majestically. "Besides, he'll need a torch."

"I'll get one," volunteered Gladys.

By the time she got back with it Thomas was breathing normally and the others were standing expectantly round the hole in the wall. It was big enough for Thomas to step through easily, but he was by no means prepared for what he found.

Lying on the floor, glinting in the beam of the torch, was a human skeleton.

A MOST CONTAGIOUS GAME

Catherine Aird

BANTAM BOOKS
TORONTO · NEW YORK · LONDON · SYDNEY

All of the characters in this book
are fictitious, and any resemblance
to actual persons, living or dead,
is purely coincidental.

A MOST CONTAGIOUS GAME
*A Bantam Book / published by arrangement with
Doubleday & Co., Inc.*

PRINTING HISTORY
*Doubleday edition published October 1967
A Selection of Mystery Guild January 1968
Bantam edition / June 1982*

*Bantam Books are published by Bantam Books, Inc. Its trade-
mark, consisting of the words ''Bantam Books'' and the por-
trayal of a rooster, is Registered in U.S. Patent and Trademark
Office and in other countries. Marca Registrada. Bantam
Books, Inc., 666 Fifth Avenue, New York, New York 10103.*

PRINTED IN THE UNITED STATES OF AMERICA

0 9 8 7 6 5 4 3 2 1

For
J.D.L. 1900-1965
who was right

It is in truth a most contagious game;
Hiding the Skeleton shall be its name.

George Meredith in *Modern Love*

One

Thomas handed over the money without demur.

Quite honestly he preferred making a straightforward donation to being made a vice-president of this or honorary member of that local society. He was unlikely ever to play bowls and quite definitely would never kick a football again, but he was a vice-president of both those clubs in Easterbrook. He would never be a choirboy either, but subscribed willingly now towards their annual outing.

"There you are, Mr. Cousens," he said to the choirmaster and organist. "Give them something special for their tea with my compliments and I hope they aren't all sick in the bus on the way home."

"It's my experience, sir," said Cousens morosely, "that they are sick on the way home whatever they have for tea."

The man was tall and thin and somewhat sour of expression. Thomas wasn't drawn to him. To be truthful, so far he had not met anyone to whom he had been drawn in Easterbrook. Certainly not the organist and choirmaster. If this was his normal appearance, this particular chap would look more at home behind the coffin rather than playing it in so to speak. Chief mourner, that was it . . . He made a conscious effort to be cheerful.

"When my works had their outings someone was always left behind and I think that's worse."

"Maybe." Nothing seemed to raise a smile with the choirmaster. "All I can say is I'm always very thankful when it's over. Thank you, sir," he added belatedly, pocketing a cheque.

Thomas Harding returned to the drawing-room. He sat down heavily and reflected that there wasn't much fun in

1

having plenty of money if you hadn't got the health to go with it. He patted his chest automatically and tried to settle in a chair, but it wasn't easy. He wasn't used to sitting in a chair in the middle of the day. He grimaced to himself. It wasn't even the middle of the day yet.

He had been through the post and read the morning papers and now there was nothing left to do. The day yawned before him, uninviting and empty, and it was barely ten o'clock in the morning. In the office he would have seen half a dozen people, dictated a dozen or more letters, surveyed his list of appointments, altered it to squeeze in a few more people, taken a handful of decisions and agreed to several more, and all by ten o'clock in the morning. This method of working had brought him as much money as he could reasonably use and a coronary thrombosis—both at the age of fifty-two.

"Quite comfortable, dear?" his wife straightened a flower in a vase as if she had entered the room for that very purpose.

"M'm," he responded absently.

"Then I think I'll pop down to the post office. You'll be all right until I come back, won't you?"

"Of course," he said testily; and then regretted it. Dora had been so good while he had been ill. "Of course I will," he said penitently. "I'll be quite happy sitting here until you come back."

It wasn't true, of course. He wasn't at all happy sitting here or anywhere else. He was bored and he had nothing to think about any longer save his heart—and he didn't really like to think about that too much. The doctors had been too emphatic for his liking. With plenty of rest, no worry and no exertion it might be years before he had another attack. Fine comfort that had been to a man who prided himself on the amount of work he could do.

As always after thinking about his illness Thomas made himself count his blessings too.

He was still alive.

He was happily married.

He was the owner of a fine manor house.

It had been one of his life's ambitions to own a really old house in the country and he had realized that if nothing else. He glanced round the drawing-room and sighed. He had meant to buy an old house all right but he had wanted to choose it himself, to find one which he could restore, to search for the sort of house he could look at and feel at once that he would like to live in.

Dora had done her best and Easterbrook Manor was very nice, of course, but it wasn't exactly what he had had in mind. It was too big to begin with and it had been restored already; at least it had plumbing of sorts and central heating of sorts. Somebody else had had a go at this room too. It was a really lovely old room but it hadn't looked like this in Queen Elizabeth's time.

He shifted irritably in the chair. He had wanted to do his own restoring, to buy a house with intangible qualities of atmosphere which couldn't be explained to a house agent. Still, Dora couldn't have known that Easterbrook Manor wouldn't have the right feel for him, and in a way it had been his own fault that it had been Dora who had to choose. It would never have happened that way if the doctor hadn't arrived unexpectedly one day to find him on the telephone to his office, his secretary taking notes by his side and his bed a mass of papers.

Dora had been dispatched next morning to the house agents with an ultimatum from the doctor and a blank cheque from him. Easterbrook Manor had been the result. On paper it had sounded ideal. A Tudor manor house with (fairly) mod. con. in an almost unspoilt village, with not too much garden and no dry rot. Lying in his centrally heated flat in London, S.W.1, Thomas Harding had felt he could not ask for more; and he bought it from his bed of sickness.

So he had come to the village of Easterbrook to retire.

Both the retirement and the village had been a disappointment so far, though he wouldn't have admitted it for worlds. The village was pretty enough and pleasant enough but the people in it were slow to greet them and Thomas missed the cheerful throng of people he knew well—of the household only Sammy, the cat, was completely settled. As for the retirement: he pursed his lips unhappily. There wasn't a great deal to be said for that if you couldn't run upstairs without getting a pain in your chest.

He hit a cushion beside him with unnecessary savagery and wondered whether it wouldn't have been better to wear out than rust out, to have ignored the doctors and gone back to his business. Then he thought of Dora and knew that that would have been wrong. Dora had been so good about leaving London and coming to Easterbrook. She had never once complained about missing her friends or the shops, or the service flat, or having a semi-invalid on her hands.

And neither would he, resolved Thomas there and then. Easterbrook Manor might be a disappointment to him but no one would ever know. He was sure it had some very good points and he would dwell on those. Take this room for instance. It was a very fine room really, even if somebody had plastered over the panelling on either side of the fireplace. A pity that. He liked the panelling. It wasn't perfect, of course, not even symmetrical, but very few of these old houses were. The ceiling dipped a bit in one corner and he was pretty sure the left-hand corner wasn't a right angle.

There was a sudden clatter behind him and Gladys, their only domestic help, staggered into the room burdened with vacuum cleaner, dusters and polish.

"I'm sorry, Mr. Harding. I didn't think you were here. You aren't in your usual chair. Can I do in here?"

"Of course, Gladys. I decided that ten o'clock was too early to sit over by the fireplace. I shall sit there this evening. I may sit in the window seat this afternoon for a change."

"That's right," she said.

"Or, of course, I could sit on the other side of the fireplace instead, but then Mrs. Harding sits there."

"That's right," said Gladys again. Thomas smiled to himself. He enjoyed irony above all; Gladys obviously did not understand it. "Then there's the study, Mr. Harding. There's lots of chairs in there."

Or did she? wondered Thomas.

"You're sure I won't disturb you? These things make a lot of noise. I could sweep it instead."

"I am quite sure, Gladys. Besides I am not doing anything so you couldn't disturb me, could you?"

Dora had once found Gladys cleaning the carpet on her hands and knees in preference to using the vacuum cleaner. Each had been unable to convince the other which method was the better but Thomas, who had dealt with trade union leaders in his time, was a great believer in avoiding trouble.

Gladys set to work with her duster and polish and Thomas looked about him. This room did not look different from here. Funny, he had never sat in this particular chair before. He really would try the window seat this afternoon after all, and perhaps the study tomorrow. That would make Dora laugh. Gladys dusted her way round the room and then unwound the vacuum wire. He wondered if he would be in her way and began to rise.

"Now don't you move, Mr. Harding. The plug is over there. Silly place for a plug, if you ask me. I'm always knocking against it."

Thomas followed her with his eyes. She was quite right.

"Whatever made them stick it right in the middle of that wall, Gladys? It must be in the way there."

"Don't ask me, Mr. Harding, but I reckon they couldn't have found a sillier place if they'd tried. Still, you know what electricians are."

"Yes," agreed Thomas hastily. No one who preferred sweeping a large carpet with a small brush to using a vacuum cleaner was likely to favour the electrical trade. "They certainly couldn't have chosen a worse place. I wonder why they did? All the other plugs and switches are all right, aren't they?"

"Yes, Mr. Harding, if you don't count the one in the larder which crackles when you turn it on."

Thomas made a mental note to have that seen to before their only daily help was electrocuted and brought his attention back to the plug in the middle of the skirting. Gladys had the vacuum cleaner on now and was going up and down the carpet with a vigour which he envied. That plug was ugly there though, and it was in the way too, sticking out like that. Perhaps if he had to get a man to mend the larder switch he could alter this one, too. His

eye swept the room. Where would be the best place?
Didn't they usually put that sort of thing near the fireplace
so that one could use an electric fire as well?

Thomas sat up. That was odd. Come to think of it, it
was rather funny that they hadn't put it by the fireplace.
You wouldn't use an electric fire right over on the opposite
skirting. He thought for a moment. His so-called study
was on the other side of the fireplace wall, and there was
an electric plug by the fireplace there. He remembered
that clearly for it was a smallish room and it heated up
quite quickly with an electric fire. Dora and he sometimes
sat in there to write letters. That was where the telephone
was. Well, why hadn't they just run the cable through the
wall and brought it out on the skirting near the fireplace?

"I'm finished now, Mr. Harding," announced Gladys, as
the whine of the vacuum died away.

"Who put the electricity in this house, Gladys? Do you
know?"

"Charlie Ford, that would be. He's the only person in
Easterbrook who would do a job like that, unless they had
a big firm come out from Calleford. But I don't think they
would. Old Mrs. Meredith didn't like doing that. I reckon
Charlie Ford would've done it, before the war, of course.
Mrs. Meredith was very up to date for all that she was an
old lady."

Thomas nodded. By Dora's standards Easterbrook
Manor was antediluvian but he knew the cottage where
Gladys lived with her old mother had neither electricity
nor indoor sanitation.

"Does—er—Charlie Ford still do electrical work?"

"Now and then," said Gladys, "but he's a builder by
rights, and undertaker of course. In between he does all
sorts of odd jobs, carpentry, glazing—you know."

Thomas knew. The sort of man who was scarcer than
gold dust in London.

"I'll get him to come to see to that switch," he said.

When Dora came back at eleven o'clock she found him
on his hands and knees on the study floor.

"It's a funny thing—," he began.

"It's not funny at all," retorted his wife. "I thought
you'd fallen."

"I'm looking at the plug socket down here in the skirting. I think the one in the big drawing-room ought to be by the fireplace instead of being stuck out on the other wall where it's in the way."

"I had noticed that," said Dora gravely, "but I hadn't expected you to."

"I've been wondering why they put it there and not by the fireplace. They could have gone through this wall here and come out by the fireplace there. Instead of that the electrician went to the trouble of running a wire all the way round the hall and along the other wall and through that. Why?"

"Perhaps he didn't think of going through this wall," said Dora.

"But he did. Look, you can see where he tried. He must have made a bit of a mess of this old skirting. He's screwed another bit of wood in—and very cleverly too."

"So he must have tried to get a wire through and failed?"

"Exactly. Now, I should like to know why he failed because I don't see why we can't have that awkward plug taken away and a power wire run through the wall into the drawing-room. It's quite simple electrically."

. Thomas rested on his heels and looked quizzically up at his wife, who smiled and said: "And you would dearly love to take out that piece of wood and see what's in the way. All right, all right, I'll fetch you a screwdriver."

Soon there was a neat hole in the skirting board and a triumphant Thomas beside it.

"I was right, Dora. Charlie Ford or whoever it was did try to run a wire through the wall. Look, you can see the hole quite easily."

"What stopped him, dear?"

"That's the odd thing. There's nothing there to stop him."

"Nothing?"

"Just space. Look at this." Thomas stooped and pulled out a long, long bean pole. "I pushed that in as far as it would go and I think I can just feel it touching something."

"But that's ridiculous. It must have come through in the drawing-room somewhere."

"No," said Thomas. But Dora had gone. He caught up with her in the drawing-room staring at the plastered wall by the fireplace.

"What does it mean, Thomas? That study wall is perfect. I would have sworn no one's touched that since the house was built. Even without half a dozen maids to polish it, it's lovely."

"The genuine patina of age," murmured Thomas. "That's what the house agent said. No, the study wall's intact. It hasn't been damaged anywhere except where that little hole was cut out at the bottom."

"This wall looks all right, too," said Dora doubtfully, peering down towards the skirting as if she still expected the bean pole to come out.

"There is something odd about it, though," said Thomas. "Something that's only just occurred to me. Those two lengths of wall on either side of the fireplace . . ."

"What about them?"

"They're plaster. The rest of the room is panelled though, just like the study."

"You mean they plastered over that lovely wood?" cried Dora. "How could they?"

"Not 'how', dear, but 'why'? That's what I'd like to know."

"But what does it mean?" asked Dora again.

Thomas shook his head. "I don't know, but if you could remember where that long measure of mine is I can probably tell you. Now, which bedrooms are above these two rooms?"

It took him nearly an hour to measure up all the rooms to his satisfaction, Dora obediently holding one end of the long measure while he wrote down figures and made calculations. When they returned to the study he seemed none the worse for the exertion.

"Well, what does all that prove?" she asked.

"A secret room."

"Thomas—not really!"

"We-e-ll, I'm almost sure," said her husband modestly.

"My workings may be wrong but I should say that there's a small room six feet by about five in between the study and the drawing-room. You don't notice it because the other side of the fireplace looks as if it's the same. It isn't really, of course. If you remember, part of the hall comes behind that and the study door."

"You'd never know from looking," protested Dora. "How clever of you to spot it."

"I've heard of these old houses having secret rooms and priest's holes," said Thomas; but he was really absurdly pleased about it himself too.

He was quite eager to get into his chair in the drawing-room the next morning and scarcely bothered with the daily paper. He wanted to check a few measurements in there and then go over his calculations before he went and had a good look at the outside of the house. It came as a complete surprise to him to hear the church clock striking noon before he had done half of what he planned.

"Thomas, there's a Mr. Ford here to see you." Dora led a large man into the room as the sound of the clock died away.

"Morning, sir. About a light switch in the larder, you said—"

"But I only asked you yesterday," said Thomas in surprise. "I didn't expect you straightaway."

The large man laughed. "Can't get used to our little country ways yet, sir? No, I didn't like the sound of that switch at all, and as your Gladys is my wife's cousin she said I was to come and see to it at once."

Thomas led him to the switch.

"Nasty," said Mr. Ford. "I should say somebody's given that a bit of a knock, wouldn't you?" He waggled it dangerously and the light flickered.

"Mr. Ford!" said Thomas suddenly. "You wouldn't be the Mr. Ford who put electricity in this house?"

"That I would, sir," said Ford easily. "In old Mrs. Meredith's day that was. Just before the war she had it done, I remember because she was so disappointed about the blackout."

"Well, let me see if you can remember anything else," said Thomas, and led him through to the study. "Do you

recollect trying to run a cable through that wall into the
drawing-room?"

Charlie Ford looked at him seriously. "That I do, Mr.
Harding. I was so sure I could that I cut a hole in the
skirting. You can see where the other wood had to be
joined in if you look carefully enough."

"Why couldn't you get through?"

"I don't know."

"You don't know!" Thomas regarded him straightly. "You
mean you tried and found you couldn't find the other wall,
is that right?"

Ford nodded.

"And you never did know why?"

The man cleared his throat. "Not rightly. You see, I was
a young man then and this was my first big job. My old
man never did take to electricity and so he left it to me. I
tried to get through that wall and I couldn't. It was one
afternoon, I recollect, and I couldn't make head nor tail of
it. All the wire I put in just disappeared and I couldn't
seem to find the drawing-room wall. Well, I thought I'd
come back next morning and have another try. My father
was out when I got home but I mentioned it to my old
Grandfather. He was proper wild about it and said that I
wasn't to try any more. He made me promise never to tell
anything about it to anybody and I never have until today."

"What about the skirting then? You fitted this wood in?"

"No, not me. That's a real craftsman's job. No, Grandfather did that. He came up with me the next morning with
a bit of real old wood he'd kept from somewhere and he
made good that hole. A carpenter of the old school he was.
He must have been turned eighty then."

"And the drawing-room plug?"

"I just ran one round the hall and through the other
wall from the dining-room. It wasn't a very good job, but
Mrs. Meredith didn't know much about electricity."

"Didn't you ever wonder about this?" demanded
Thomas, pointing to the hole in the skirting.

"Plenty of times," retorted Ford, "but come 1939 I was
in the Army, and when I came out Grandfather was dead
and Mrs. Meredith was dead and the people that were

here always had a firm from Calleford do their work and I sort of lost interest."

Thomas saw the point of that. He had been in business himself.

"I reckoned the old gaffer knew something about this all right and that he hadn't told my father and he didn't want me to know either."

Thomas nodded. "And I reckon there's a secret room in between this wall and that of the drawing-room." He produced his pieces of paper. "I've measured the bedrooms above here and they are six feet longer and I can get a six foot bean pole in that hole you made."

"Can't be anything else from them figures," said Charlie Ford at last, tapping Thomas's paper with a stubby finger. "I wonder who put it there?"

"I think it's probably as old as the house. No, what I should like to know is—who plastered up the wall in the drawing-room."

The two men walked into the other room and stood looking at the plastered wall beside the fireplace. Charlie Ford ran his hand professionally along the junction with the skirting.

"Well, it's fairly old plaster. It was here when I tried to get that wire through." He tapped it carefully, as a doctor taps a chest. "I should say there's panelling behind it, just like the rest of the room."

"Would you say, Mr. Ford," said Dora, coming in behind them, "that it would be very difficult to take the plaster down to see?"

"Easiest job in the world, Mrs. Harding," said Charlie Ford eagerly. "I could start first thing tomorrow morning."

Dora nearly laughed aloud at his enthusiasm, while Thomas gave her a look compounded of gratitude and such pure joy that she hadn't seen since his illness.

Charlie Ford was as good as his word and turned up with a lad next morning. The lad was small but eager. Shrimp-like, he stood one pace behind the burly Ford. Thomas looked at him, seeing not a builder's lad but himself forty years ago. Would this boy find streets paved with gold?

"Now you just sit there and keep an eye on me," said

Charlie Ford kindly. Gladys had told his wife all about Mr. Harding's bad heart. Thomas established himself in his chair and watched the big man strip the wall.

"There's the panelling," he said after a while. The exposed wood was white and discoloured from the plaster but of the same design as the rest of the room. The lad was kept busy tidying up the fallen plaster. He was unlucky enough to have Gladys supervising at this as well as Charlie Ford.

Thomas wasn't worried about the plaster, though. It was the panelling which interested him. As the day wore on more and more of this could be seen and Dora began to regret her impetuous suggestion. The wood might never polish properly. She slid into a chair beside Thomas.

"Isn't it exciting, dear?" she began obliquely.

"It's getting behind that panelling that will be exciting," he said. "And I don't know how to do it. I don't want to break it down but I do want to get into the room."

Charlie Ford heard this last and came across. "We'll have this clear by tomorrow, Mr. Harding. What do we do then? Force it?"

"Not if you can help it. There's no door visible, is there?"

"Can't even see a crack. Come and look for yourself."

Thomas felt the panelling all over. There was nothing to suggest an entrance.

Charlie Ford and his lad had the rest of the plaster cleared by eleven o'clock the next day. Gladys was lending them a hand with the dust and Thomas and Dora were examining the panelling when Dora gave a little cry.

"It moved. I'm sure it moved," she said.

"Where were you touching?" asked Thomas, while Charlie Ford put his heavy hand alongside Dora's.

"Here, Mr. Harding. I felt it too."

Thomas ducked under the builder's arms, his fingers running feverishly over the old wood.

"There's a crack coming," he croaked excitedly. "Push man, push."

Charlie Ford heaved his portly frame at the panelling while Dora pressed her hands into the crack Thomas found.

"Harder, Mr. Ford, harder. I've got my knuckles in now."

The crack was soon wide enough for Thomas's hand, too, and then they were all tugging at a sliding panel.

"It's coming," squeaked the lad. "It's nearly open."

"Whew! That was hard work," said Thomas, sinking breathlessly into a chair. There was a large square hole in the wall now.

"Aren't you going to look inside, Mr. Harding?" asked the builder's boy. He could hardly stand still with excitement.

"Give him time to get his breath back, lad," commanded Charlie Ford majestically. "Besides, he'll need a torch."

"I'll get one," volunteered Gladys.

By the time she got back with it Thomas was breathing normally and the others were standing expectantly round the hole in the wall. It was big enough for Thomas to step through easily enough but he was by no means prepared for what he found.

Lying on the floor, glinting in the beam of the torch, was a human skeleton.

Two

ONE by one they all stepped into the secret room and peered at the skeleton by torchlight.

"I haven't a measure with me," declared Charlie Ford professionally, "but I would say that hadn't been . . . wasn't . . . a very tall person."

Dora shuddered. She had forgotten Charlie was the local undertaker as well. Nevertheless she, too, climbed in beside her husband to see their macabre find. Thomas had been right about the size of the room. There was plenty of space for them both and the skeleton. It lay on the floor across the narrower side of the room.

"Poor thing," cried Dora involuntarily. "Did it get trapped in here and suffocate do you think?"

"It certainly didn't suffocate," said Thomas. "The air in here is quite fresh. It could have starved to death."

He looked at the whitened bones and wondered how they could possibly tell.

"That would be worse—so much slower," said Dora compassionately. Thomas ushered her out and looked enquiringly at Gladys.

"I don't really want to look, Mr. Harding, but I think I'd better. Mother will want to know all about it." For which surprising reason she hitched up her overall and stepped through the hole in the panelling. Whether her first sight of a human skeleton stunned her into silence or whether she was memorizing the scene for later description, Thomas couldn't tell. All she said as she returned to the live company in the drawing-room was, "I think I'll make a cup of tea."

"Can I see it please," Mr. Ford?" The builder's lad was hopping about on tip-toe behind them.

"Now why should an honest-to-God skeleton interest ou?" demanded Charlie Ford. "It's got nothing on them orror films you waste your time on."

"Oh, please, Mr. Ford. I've never seen a real skeleton efore."

"All right then, in you go, you bloodthirsty little brute." Ie waited until the boy reappeared and then said leasantly, "I reckon you and that skeleton would be about he same size. Now if you was to lay down in there beside t I could tell for sure."

The boy, slightly paler now, was saved from this by Gladys and a tray of tea. Thomas took a cup gratefully. A ecret room was one thing but a skeleton in it was another.

Charlie Ford declared it was a police matter, and Dora hought they ought to have a doctor, too. Thomas sent for oth to be on the safe side. The doctor's wife reported that er husband would be most interested in a skeleton and vould be round as soon as a baby case was over.

"The post office," observed Gladys. "Their first."

The policeman responded by turning up in person on nis bicycle so quickly that he must have pedalled downhill us well as up. He was even in time for a cup of tea.

"Better have it while it's hot, Jack Wilkins," advised Gladys. "It'll be cold by the time you've seen them bones."

"They've been there long enough," said Charlie Ford. 'A few more minutes won't make a lot of difference."

"As a matter of interest," said Thomas, feeling an obscure need to assert himself, "how long does it take for a body to—er—you know—get like that?"

P.c. Wilkins set down his cup. "About a year and a half if it's exposed to the air, about twice as long in the water and about ten if it's buried in ordinary soil."

"Twelve," said Charlie Ford, the undertaker.

P.c. Wilkins did not argue the point. His experience of bodies was more limited than he cared for the others to know.

"Then this skeleton could be quite—well—new?" said Dora doubtfully.

"No, it couldn't, Mrs. Harding," said Charlie Ford firmly. "You see this plaster was here when I was a lad like

I told your husband. Besides, that plaster's old. You ca
tell. They don't make stuff like that these days."

"Can we begin at the beginning, please?" P.c. Wilki
unbuttoned his tunic pocket and felt for his notebook.

Between them they told him the story of the electricit
the plaster and the panelling, and Thomas showed him h
drawings and calculations.

"I'll keep those for the time being, sir, if I may." Th
constable looked round the five of them. "You've all bee
in and had a look, I suppose. . . ."

"Naturally," said Charlie Ford stoutly. "Why?"

"Footprints," said Wilkins. "Now, if I might see the-
er—deceased."

He reappeared about five minutes later.

"Well, Mr. Harding, I can't tell you how long it's bee
there nor who it was, but I can tell you two things . . ." h
paused impressively, " . . . I can tell you that whoever
was, was murdered."

Thomas nodded his head slowly. "I was afraid of that.

"Not starved nor suffocated?" said Dora.

"Hit very hard on the back of the head with a blun
instrument," announced P.c. Wilkins succinctly. "The sku
is fractured. You can just see it without touching th
body."

"Poor thing," said Dora again.

"You said you could tell two things," Thomas reminde
him. "What was the other?"

"That he wasn't murdered in there. There isn't room t
swing a weapon far enough to break a skull."

"I hadn't thought of that," said Thomas approvingly.

Wilkins shut his notebook. "I'll have to let Callefor
know about this."

He was back again before luncheon was cleared away
this time with a tall, lean man, older than himself.

"And this is Inspector Bream from Calleford."

Thomas shook hands with him. He had a firm, decide
grip. There would be no time wasted by this man.

Bream nodded affably. "Nasty surprise for you, sir. I
was a surprise, I take it?"

"Indeed it was," Thomas assured him, and repeated th
story of the discovery.

Both policemen went in the secret room and Thomas could hear the odd rumble as they spoke but not very clearly. That panelling must be thick and well fitting. Then the police photographer arrived, hung about with as much equipment as the White Knight. His lanky companion he took to be the fingerprint man. He ushered them to the hole feeling very much like a museum curator. There wasn't room for them all inside and P.c. Wilkins clambered out while the photographer got to work.

"What will happen now?" asked Thomas.

"As soon as we've got all our photographs and fingerprints we'll move the body for a post-mortem."

"And then?"

"Then we start to trace the murderer," said the policeman seriously.

Inspector Bream had a notebook too. He wanted to put in it what had made Thomas decide to come to Easterbrook Manor. Thomas gave him the names of the estate agents and the previous owner.

"That's right," confirmed Wilkins. "They were called Smith when they came but Smythe by the time they left. London people they were. The house stood empty a long time before it was sold but I don't suppose they told you that, Mr. Harding."

"Why was it empty so long?" said the Inspector sharply.

"On account of the price. I heard it was a bit steep," said the constable uncomfortably, not looking at Thomas.

"It was," said Thomas simply, "but the value of something is what the purchaser is prepared to pay and what the seller is prepared to accept at one and the same time."

This gem of business philosophy was lost on the Inspector who said suspiciously, "You mean you paid more than the house was worth?"

"At the time I needed somewhere out of London to live and I wanted an old house," responded Thomas mildly. "I paid them what they asked and what the house was worth to me."

"Did you know these people Smith or Smythe?"

"I never met them. My solicitors handled the negotiations for me with their agents." He had not particularly wanted to meet them; but just because they indulged in suburban snobbery and had overcharged him on their house didn't indicate them to be murderers as well.

"I dare say we can contact them easily enough," said the Inspector. "How long was the house empty, Wilkins?"

"About a year, sir."

"Long enough for a fair bit of dirty work," said Thomas reflectively.

"Hardly long enough for the body to decay though," put in Wilkins.

The Inspector favoured him with a repressive look. "Have you any Missing Persons in Easterbrook, Constable?"

"Not answering to that description," Wilkins inclined his head to the secret room.

"Oh, and to what description do your Missing Persons answer?" demanded the Inspector dangerously.

"Female, aged nineteen, five foot six, brunette, last seen very much alive last Saturday week when her parents refused her permission to marry. Now believed to be living in Calleford."

Thomas studied the carpet carefully.

"And you, sir, can tell us nothing more?"

"Nothing," said Thomas regretfully. "I bought Easterbrook Manor out of the blue and came here to retire. I discovered there was a secret room there quite by chance and had no idea there would be a skeleton in it."

"Well, the pathologist will want to look at it *in situ* so to speak, and then we'll take it away. You'll be hearing from us again, sir."

On which rather depressing note the police posse took their leave.

"Well, are we to be arrested?" enquired Dora, coming into the room with afternoon tea.

"Is that the time? What? Oh, no, I don't think so, but they're going to talk to the Smythes."

"They didn't behave," said Dora drily, "as if they wanted to get rid of the house in a hurry."

"We got an extra room into the bargain though, so perhaps it wasn't such a bad buy after all."

"You haven't made many of those, have you, dear?"

"What?"

"Bad buys. Who's this coming up the drive now?"

Thomas turned his head. "The doctor. I'd forgotten all about him."

"A boy. Both well," they heard him say briefly to Gladys as he reached the drawing-room. "Ah, Mr. Harding, you've got a skeleton I hear. Where?"

Dr. Curzan was in his early forties and rather too brisk for Thomas's liking; but then Thomas himself had been brisk enough in his own forties. It would be no use warning the doctor of the danger of overwork, and anyway Thomas had only met him half a dozen times and then at the other end of a stethoscope. He had been disappointingly noncommittal on these occasions.

"Over here," he said equally briefly and led the way to the hole in the panelling.

Thomas held the torch while the doctor made his examination.

"Well, it's male and not adult," he said at once.

Thomas peered over his shoulder, interested in his rapid decision. "How do you know?"

"The epiphyseal cartilages are still present at the knee and elbow joints. They disappear in the long bones in the areas nearest the elbow and knee joints by the age of twenty-one, and they are the last in the body to go." He peered closely at the skeleton's feet. "All the other epiphyseal cartilages disappear before these go. There's no further growth you see once they are united."

Thomas did not see but did not say so. Instead he asked how old he thought the man had been.

"I can't tell you the exact age but there are ways of telling. It's scarcely a man, you know, a boy more likely."

"It's not very tall," agreed Thomas doubtfully. "Charlie Ford noticed that."

This appeared to amuse the doctor. "There *are* other ways of measuring skeletons than Charlie Ford's practised eye, of course. There's Pearson's formula."

"Pearson's formula?"

"It's a mathematical formula by which you can work out the height of a body given the length of one of the long bones."

"But who would want to murder a boy?"

"Couldn't say." Dr. Curzan was studying another bone

now. "I can't tell you when it died but you've nothing to worry about. Look, the periosteum's all gone and the bone is beginning to crumble."

Thomas looked. He didn't know what the periosteum was but if it wasn't there he couldn't see it anyway. "That means that this is pretty old then, doesn't it?"

"Myself, I should say well over a hundred years—nearer two probably—but I'm no expert. Cause of death: fractured skull with no evidence to show how it happened. It'll need a postmortem of course."

Thomas nodded. The man might be brisk but he certainly knew his stuff. Dr. Curzan dusted his trouser knees, and together they went back into the daylight.

"I used to like anatomy," said the doctor reflectively. "You always knew where you were with anatomy."

"What more can the chap who does the post-mortem tell?"

"The pathologist? Oh, he can probably estimate the age at death pretty accurately and how old the skeleton is."

"Wonderful how they do it, isn't it?"

"Not really," said the general practitioner casually. "Take the odontoid process of the axis for instance. Now that is usually ossified by the age of twelve. The pathologist will get a good look at that—if it's not damaged of course. That must have been a nasty smack on the head by the way. Then there are the bone sutures—he'll get some X rays of those. The teeth tell you a lot. Did you notice the teeth?"

Thomas nodded. "Hideous, weren't they? A full set grinning away."

That aspect did not appear to have struck the doctor. "The teeth were interesting. The wisdom teeth hadn't erupted and there was no sign of obvious decay."

"I had no idea teeth were so big."

"The gum covers more than you'd think. If I had to hazard a guess I'd say that's the body of a lad of about fourteen or fifteen."

The doctor was on his way out when he remembered to ask how Thomas was.

"Fine, thank you." If nothing else, he could thank the secret room for the way in which the last three days had flown.

Thomas found the pathologist who arrived later uncommunicative and cheerless. He brought his own torch and assistant with him. They went into the secret room and stayed there almost an hour. When they emerged the pathologist said he would be sending for the skeleton in the morning and took his leave.

Thomas went back to his chair and stared at the hole in the panelling. If the doctor was right these remains were old, and if Charlie Ford was right about the plaster that was old, too. In that case how did Charlie's grandfather know about the room? Thomas did a bit of rapid mental arithmetic. Charlie's grandfather couldn't have been born earlier than—say—1855 so what could he have known about a secret room containing an old skeleton walled up, in all probability, fifty years before he was born? But he had known something about the secret room. Thomas was sure about that. The skirting board in the study had been most carefully repaired to stop anyone noticing that it had been touched; and in any case why swear his grandson to secrecy?

It was all very odd.

He cast his mind back to Charlie Ford's behaviour. There had been nothing in it to suggest that he didn't want the room found, or even that he knew it was there. Quite the reverse really, thought Thomas. He had been eager and willing to strip the plaster down.

The plaster: now surely there was something which could be checked? He went out through the back of the house and sure enough there was an untidy heap of it lying by the coal shed. Builders were the same the world over. Thomas selected a largish piece and put it in his study drawer. It looked very much like other plaster to him save that there were horsehairs sticking out of it. That didn't mean a lot but it did prove that the room hadn't been walled up last year.

The skeleton was collected very early the next morning, well before Thomas was about. He spent his morning examining the secret room properly, something he couldn't bring himself to do while the skeleton was there. The pathetic collection of bones drew the human eye away from anything else.

The room was six feet long and some five feet wide. Two of its walls were wood, being the other side of the panelled walls of the study and drawing-room; they lacked polish but they were of the same stout oak. The other two sides were of brick, one the outer wall of the house and the other side of the chimney. A primitive drain ran away in a corner under the thick outside wall of the Manor. There would be room enough here for a fugitive to live and sleep—if not in comfort, at least without hardship. The chimney would provide warmth in winter and some- where there was ventilation. Quite good ventilation, de- cided Thomas, breathing deeply. It must have been good anyway for the skeleton to have decayed without being discovered all these years ago.

"Thomas, where are you?"

Dora's voice, coming from the drawing-room, was muf- fled but audible. He poked his head out of the panelling.

"Ah, there you are," she said. "What are you doing?"

"Having a good look at our priest's hole."

"Was it one?"

"I don't know, but whoever built it made a good job of it."

"But the skeleton," said Dora doubtfully, "wasn't all that old, was it? Two hundred years, didn't the doctor say?"

"He did. But this room's as old as the house. A built-in refuge, rather like we built air-raid shelters. It was planned for someone to be able to live here for quite a while."

"Do you suppose they hung a portrait on the wall out here?"

"What for?"

"So that whoever was in here could look out through the eyes of the portrait," said Dora. "I saw it in a film once, but the man spoilt it by winking."

"I hadn't thought about that," said Thomas seriously. "There must have been some sort of peephole."

It took him over an hour to find it. At last, standing on a kitchen chair, his fingers fastened on what could have been a knot in the wood, high up in the wall. Only it wasn't a knot in the wood. It was a small hole. Thomas applied his eyes to this and found himself looking down on to the study table. He stepped down from his perch and hurried through into the study. Even though he knew where to look, it was several minutes before he spotted the hole. The centre of an ornamental Tudor rose was missing. That was all. The tiny round centre of the carving was gone and there was a scarcely noticeable dark hole where it had been.

"Clever," he murmured. "Very clever."

He found a similar device in the drawing-room wall, though that had been plastered up and was more difficult to shift. Through this second hole he could see Dora arranging a bowl of flowers in the drawing-room and talking to Gladys. He put his ear to the hole instead of his eye and heard them talking quite clearly about luncheon.

It wasn't until four o'clock that the police called again, this time in the person of Constable Wilkins. He was alone.

"Inspector Bream thought you would be interested in the pathologist's report," he said unenthusiastically.

"Of course," said Thomas. "I've been waiting for it."

P.c. Wilkins opened his notebook. "The skeleton was of a male person aged between fifteen and sixteen at the time of death, which was approximately one hundred and fifty years ago. Cause of death: fracture of skull." He sighed heavily.

"That's the gist of it, Mr. Harding. There's a couple of pages of it but that's what it boils down to."

"What happens now?" Dora wanted to know.

"Well, the coroner has been informed and he'll have to hold an inquest I suppose. And that is all there is to it. They'll have an open verdict."

"But it's murder," protested Dora. "Somebody killed the poor boy. Aren't the police going to find out who?"

"No, madam. You see the murderer's dead by now."

Thomas grinned sympathetically. He guessed from the policeman's manner that he had already had all this out with the Inspector.

"Never mind, Constable," he said cheerfully. "I'm sure this isn't the only murder in the county. You'll just have to be patient."

Three

Four days later Thomas came down to breakfast immaculate in his City uniform of black jacket and striped trousers. Dora raised her eyebrows enquiringly.

"The inquest," said Thomas reproachfully. "You hadn't forgotten, had you?"

Thomas had in fact received a subpoena to attend, but wild horses would not have kept him away. He was highly curious to know what the due processes of the law would decide about this skeleton.

"I didn't think my country things would do," he said, looking down with pleasure at his spotless cuffs. Since coming to Easterbrook Manor, Thomas had affected what he was pleased to call rough tweeds, but these were of so fine a cloth and so mild a pattern that Gladys was wont to describe them to her mother as "a bit dull for a man".

"Certainly not," agreed Dora. "Besides, I've always liked you in black."

Indeed Thomas looked every inch the City gentleman as he stood before the coroner to depose how he found the skeleton. The inquest was held in the Calleford Guildhall, an ancient timbered building once the pride of the city and still a reminder of the medieval importance of the place. The dark oak beams and benches lent an air of sombre solemnity to the proceedings. Her Majesty's Coroner was a wizened little man who was, Thomas gathered, a local solicitor. He listened carefully to what Thomas said, but asked him no questions. Against the backcloth of black oak he looked ageless and remote.

Inspector Bream brought the atmosphere back to the present with a start by his description of the secret room

and an account of the enquiries he had made of the
previous owners, the Templeton-Smythes.

The coroner scratched away with his pen.

"With a hyphen?" he asked.

The Inspector nodded. "Yes, sir. They are living in
London now. . . ."

"That will have something to do with it," agreed the
coroner drily.

"But they knew nothing of the room or its contents, and
in view of the pathologist's report I did not pursue these
enquiries further."

"Thank you, Inspector," said the coroner courteously,
and waited with no visible impatience while the pathologist identified himself and took the oath.

Much of his evidence was incomprehensible to Thomas,
but slowly a picture emerged of the human being to whom
the skeleton had belonged. In dry, academic phrases the
pathologist explained exactly why he was of the opinion
that the deceased had been a male aged between fifteen
and sixteen years at the time of death. With a wealth of
technical detail he told the coroner that death had occurred some one hundred and fifty to two hundred years
earlier; and then with a simplicity which stilled the room
he declared that death was due to a fracture of a skull.

"Thank you, Doctor. I am, of course, only a layman,"
here the coroner coughed deprecatingly, "but can you tell
me why the body did not—um—mummify? We have been
told it was in an enclosed room next to a big chimney and
I understand—um—that dry warmth constitutes—er—
favourable circumstances."

"The ventilation of the room was so good as to repro-
duce the atmosphere not of the house but of the outside
air, sir." The pathologist had his answer ready. "On the day
that I examined the body my assistant found the humidity
of the room in which it lay to be the same as that out of
doors. That of the rest of the house was considerably less.
I did not examine the room closely but I should imagine
there to be several air ducts from the outside wall. No
doubt the police found them."

There was no doubt from Inspector Bream's face that
the police had not found them.

"As you will be aware, sir, a body will not mummify in the ordinary atmosphere."

"Thank you, Doctor, please go on."

"I found no evidence to show how the skull was fractured, but it is unlikely that so serious an injury could have been inflicted within the confines of so small a room, accidentally or otherwise."

The coroner nodded.

"In support of this," concluded the pathologist, "is the fact that the hands of the skeleton had been folded across the chest after death and the fingers interlocked."

On which macabre note he stood down. Thomas regarded him with respect. He might be a cold-blooded fellow but he hadn't missed much.

The coroner scratched away with his pen for a few moments and then looked up.

"I find that the deceased met his death from a fracture of the skull and that there is insufficient evidence to show how this was inflicted. I shall therefore adjourn this inquest *sine die*."

Thomas met Inspector Bream in the corridor.

"Well, that's that, Mr. Harding. Your worries are over now."

"I can't say I'm not disappointed, Inspector. I thought you people were always interested in murder. I looked to you to solve this one."

"Solve a murder that happened two hundred years ago! Even if we did solve it there would be nobody to arrest, would there? Be reasonable, Mr. Harding. I wouldn't even know where to begin. Our Missing Persons list doesn't go back that far you know." He smiled thinly. "You heard how up to date Constable Wilkins's was."

"It's still murder," said Thomas obstinately.

"It could have been murder," corrected the Inspector. "It could have been an accident—things were different in those days."

"A man wouldn't plaster up a room with a body in it if it was an accident," argued Thomas, "nor push a dead body into a secret room in the first place if it had died by falling off a haystack or down a flight of stairs."

"You may be right, Mr. Harding. All I can say is that I'm

thankful I don't have to prove anything. I've got another dead body on my hands at the moment and it's one that I know a great deal too much about for somebody's comfort."

"You know a lot about mine," persisted Thomas. "Age, sex, cause of death and more or less when he died."

"I know all that about this other body, too," said the Inspector gently, "and, what is more, I know her name as well and I shall soon know for certain who killed her. In the meantime it's keeping me pretty busy."

With which Thomas had to be content.

The next morning he settled himself in his chair, but he did so willingly. He wasn't a prisoner condemned to a day's fruitless idleness but a man with some thinking ahead of him. Gladys was doing the room and he watched her polishing the newly uncovered panelling. It was still white from the plaster and she was making little headway.

"It's not coming up very well, Mr. Harding." She paused, red with exertion.

"It's got about two hundred years to catch up with the rest you know."

Gladys stared critically at the wood. "I can give it half an hour every morning," she said helpfully. "Mr. Harding, Jack Wilkins says that skeleton was ever so old."

"It was, Gladys. About two hundred years."

"Was it put there when the house was built?"

"Oh, no, the house is much older than that, about four hundred years old."

"Well, why has it got a secret room then?"

Thomas took a deep breath. He didn't know very much English history. He had had quite a struggle even to get his foot on the bottom rung of the ladder to success; and he had left school long before being taught details of the Elizabethan period.

"I think it was for a priest to hide in."

"Oh, a Roman Catholic," sniffed Gladys. "There's a lot of them over Cullingoak way. A convent, you know. What was he hiding for?"

"I think Queen Elizabeth was persecuting the Catholics at the time," said Thomas, who was not at all sure.

"They weren't still hiding when our skeleton got in there?"

"No," said Thomas hurriedly. "They were quite free then."

Or were they? he wondered.

"Come to think of it," said Gladys, gathering up her dusters, "our skeleton was a boy, wasn't it, so he couldn't have been a priest, could he?"

Thomas watched her go. Already to her it was "our" skeleton. He grinned to himself. He had begun to think of it that way himself. The police certainly didn't feel any pride of possession in it. Thomas was sorry about that. He had been hoping that they would tell him who that poor bundle of bones had been, how and why it had met its death. With these wonderfully scientific methods of detection he had had greater hopes of a solution than he had admitted.

"I forgot the polish, Mr. Harding." Gladys came back again. "Oh, Mother was asking when we should know about the skeleton. What shall I tell her?"

"Gladys, one of these days I should like to meet your mother."

"I'm sure Mother would be very pleased, Mr. Harding. What shall I say about the skeleton?"

"I'm afraid you'll have to tell her the police aren't going to do anything about it so we shall never know who it was now."

He said much the same thing to Dora at lunch time.

"What I can't understand is who would want to kill a young boy like that," said Dora.

"There are always reasons enough for murder," said her husband practically. "Fear, greed, jealousy. Just plain anger sometimes."

"But not a boy, Thomas. He was scarcely more than a child."

"The little Princes in the Tower *were* children and someone murdered them."

"And the police aren't interested?"

"Not any more. They say they have another murder on their hands, more up to date than mine."

"That'll be the Calleford blonde," said Dora unexpectedly.

"The what?"

"The Calleford blonde."

"And who is the Calleford blonde?"

"I don't know," admitted Dora, "but that is what the newspaper reporter who spoke to the milkman who found her called her. He said it would make a good headline, and the milkman told Gladys's mother. Strangling, I think it was."

"Does Gladys's mother ever go out?" asked Thomas.

"Never," said Dora. "She's got arthritis. Why?"

"I only wondered."

"They found her—the Calleford blonde, I mean—early yesterday morning. The police are working on the murder now."

"I know," said Thomas plaintively, "but really my murder is much more interesting. I can think of several reasons for strangling a blonde but none for fracturing the skull of a boy of fifteen."

"Or why Charlie Ford's grandfather should have known about the room. And it's odd that old Mrs. Meredith, whoever she was, shouldn't have known about the room if Charlie's grandfather did."

"It is, isn't it," agreed Thomas absently. "Dora, you realise that that wall couldn't have been plastered up without the owner knowing? So whoever was living here when that boy died knew all about it."

"Unless there was a tenant."

"Any owner would want to know why a tenant did some unnecessary plastering," retorted Thomas, who had been a landlord in his time. "In any case, the owner would presumably know about the secret room, and if a tenant blocked it up, would want to know the reason why. No, the owner would have done this and done it knowing that there was a body inside."

"Why couldn't one person have put the body in at one time and another done the plastering years later without looking inside?"

Thomas thought for a moment. "I don't think the legend of a secret room would die out quickly enough. This room was put in when the house was built. I don't suppose it was ever used much after Queen Elizabeth died, do you? That awful woman who came before Elizabeth . . . what was she called? There's a cocktail or something named after her . . ."

"Bloody Mary."

"That's her. Well she was all in favour of priests, wasn't she? So surely they didn't need to hide after Elizabeth."

"Oliver Cromwell?" said Dora tentatively.

"I'd forgotten about him. Well, say it wasn't used after the Civil War then. We know the body was put in it— well—more than a hundred years after that. It would have needed another couple of generations at least to forget so completely about the room as to plaster it over by accident."

"The house could have been sold," Dora pointed out.

"Even so the local people would have remembered. Can't you see them rushing up to afternoon tea . . ."

"Not tea, dear. That's new."

"Port wine then, or what's that stuff you used to take with seed cake?"

"Madeira."

"Can't you see them rushing up anyway, and asking if they'd found the secret room?"

"Not so very secret," observed Dora.

"But there would be no need for a secret room then, would there? The shape of danger had altered. Didn't we do our fighting abroad after that?" said Thomas vaguely.

"So whoever plastered over the wood knew about the room and the body . . ."

"And the body. That's why they put the plaster up. If it had been just for decoration they would have plastered all the panelling over."

"Oh, they wouldn't!" protested Dora. "Not all that beautiful wood."

"I have always understood," said Thomas darkly, "that the Victorians were capable of anything."

"Well then, haven't we just got to find the owner at the time to find the murderer?"

Thomas folded his napkin and said mildly, "A slight oversimplification, my dear. Even if we found the owner at the time we shan't know who the boy was and why he was killed. Or even exactly when—the pathologist gave a fairly wide range of dates, you know." He pushed his chair back. "I could get them to send the deeds of the house down from town, I suppose."

"Do. I should like to be sure the Templeton-Smythes hadn't been here since time immemorial." Dora smiled sweetly and Thomas went off chuckling to write to his solicitors.

After breakfast the next day Thomas said what a nice morning it was. A few moments later he reminded his wife that Dr. Curzan had said a little gentle exercise would do his heart no harm, and as she was collecting up her letters he remarked casually that he had thought of walking to the village.

Dora entered into the spirit of this by asking him to buy some stamps if he were near the post office, and with her tacit approval of his outing he set off.

Half an hour later Mr. Martindale, the Rector of Easterbrook, came across him in the churchyard rubbing some moss off the gravestone of a blacksmith who died in 1789.

"Good morning," said Thomas. "Lovely day."

The Rector agreed it was—for the time of the year, and leant forward to read the inscription on the stone.

"Ah, the village blacksmith. An important man in a village in those days."

"I wasn't looking for him," said Thomas.

"No?" said the Rector politely.

"No, I was looking for the old owners of the Manor. Would they be here by any chance?"

"My dear chap," said the cleric warmly, "they are indeed. There are lots of them. Barbarys, mostly. You're looking in the wrong place. They're mostly in the church."

The Rector set off across the churchyard, nipping carefully round ancient and modern graves and between old, old yew trees. He went through the porch into the church and down the side aisle. He came to rest before a worn stone in the floor marking the tomb of a certain Sir Tobias Barbary, 1st Baronet, who had been called to his fathers in 1605.

"Here's the fellow you want." He tapped the gravestone informally. "Sir Tobias Barbary of Easterbrook. He's the earliest Barbary, and his son is over there, and *his* son is under that stone there. There's a couple of them the other side of the font and then one of them built a family vault. Come out and have a look at it. You'll be interested in them, of course," added the Rector obliquely over his shoulder.

"Well, it's not everyone who finds a skeleton in their drawing-room," admitted Thomas. "I did wonder if I would find any of them here at all. I thought a priest's hole would mean they were Catholics."

"It might mean that whoever built the house were Catholics. The Barbarys certainly weren't or they wouldn't be here." The Rector wrinkled his forehead. "I had an idea they didn't build Easterbrook Manor, you know. They must have bought it fairly soon after it was built though. It's undoubtedly Tudor."

Thomas nodded. He had had that in writing from the estate agents.

Dora came across them both an hour later deep in contemplation before the memorial to the last Barbary in the churchyard, one Sir Walter Barbary, 10th Baronet, who died ("in sure and certain hope of the Resurrection that is to come") early in 1870; she greeted the Rector and bore Thomas home.

"I thought I'd find you there," she murmured.

"It was a man called Barbary," said Thomas hurriedly, "or to be more accurate, a baronet called Barbary. The church is full of them and their relics."

"And which of them was here at the time of the skeleton?"

Thomas opened his notebook. "There was a Sir Toby who died in 1748, a Sir Toby who died in 1799, and another Sir Toby who was killed at the Battle of Waterloo. He was the eighth baronet, then there was the ninth, Sir Richard, he died in 1835. There's only one more after that anyway. Sir Walter, the 10th Baronet, who died in 1870. You saw his grave."

Dora frowned. "So there are four possibilities—the sixth, seventh, eighth and ninth baronets."

"That's right, though the sixth is a bit on the early side to be likely. The pathologist said a hundred and fifty to two hundred years. Sir Richard was the public benefactor one, whose tablet was above the pew where we sat. Do you remember?"

They had both noticed it at the time. The memorial was just above the pew to which they had been shown on the occasion of their first visit to the church. In the weeks that followed Thomas had complained that Sir Richard wasn't the only public benefactor: it was extraordinary the number of village societies that wanted to welcome him as a vice-president.

"So it must have been one of the four who had that wall plastered over," said Dora thoughtfully.

"Yes, and that one must have known about the skeleton."

He amused himself that afternoon by drawing up a list of the Barbarys he had found in the church, and churchyard.

"That's funny," said Dora, when she saw it. "They start off as Tobias and then they change to Toby but they are all called one or the other until that one who died in 1835."

"Perhaps there was no heir and it passed to a brother."

"Well you'd think he would call his son Toby, wouldn't you, just for tradition's sake. He didn't, did he?"

"No, his son was called Walter. The Victorians may not have cared about that sort of thing though."

"Nonsense," declared Dora roundly. "When the name goes all that way back too. Now, how do we tell which of the four it was?"

Thomas laughed. "My dear, I don't suppose we will ever know. We'll just have to be content with knowing that it was probably one of those four."

The next thing that happened at Easterbrook Manor was the apparently irrelevant invitation of Dora to afternoon tea with the Misses Siskin.

The Misses Siskin had called formally on Thomas and Dora when they moved to the Manor and Dora had, with no little trepidation, returned the call. Now she had been invited to tea. Thomas, who had most ungallantly prolonged his afternoon rest the day they called, was not included in the invitation.

"And you've no business to look so pleased about it," said Dora severely.

On the other hand Gladys had been very impressed when she heard about the invitation.

"Ever so old they are," she volunteered, "but proper gentry. It isn't everyone they have there, Mrs. Harding. Miss Maud's the one with the lorgnette by the way. They didn't half used to frighten me when I was little."

"They frighten me too," Dora confided to Thomas before setting out. "I wish you were coming."

"I must have my rest," said Thomas virtuously. "You go and enjoy yourself."

"Beast," said his spouse pleasantly.

She was back again in two hours quite excited. "I've had such an interesting time..."

"I thought you didn't want to go," said Thomas.

"I didn't but they talked about the Barbarys. That Sir Walter—"

"Died 1870, Tenth Baronet."

"Him—or is it he? Anyway, that one. He wasn't the last, but he had no son so the title passed to his cousin in America. They think he had a son and a grandson at the time but they never came back to Easterbrook. They sold the property when they inherited, and since then the house has changed hands about a dozen times."

"That's interesting," said Thomas.

"I've had the life history of all the twelve owners since Sir Walter, I think," said Dora. "That pair remember nearly all of them. And those they didn't know themselves they still know all about because their mother knew them."

"Did they know about the secret room?"

"They were terribly correct—they didn't even mention the skeleton."

"Perhaps they didn't know."

"Not know! I should think they know all about everybody in Easterbrook."

"Do they know why this house has had so many owners since then?"

"Only that none of them really seemed to settle." She hesitated. "Thomas . . ."

"Yes?"

"Thomas, you don't think there was a reason, do you?"

"If you mean is the house haunted," said Thomas equably, "then the answer is no. What is interesting is that there was a baronet after that Sir Walter who died in 1870."

"Oh, I nearly forgot," cried Dora. "They lent me this." She produced a small book, limp bound, the gold lettering faded into illegibility. After a moment Thomas made out the date 1885 on the cover, and the word "Baronetage" on the spine. He stirred excitedly in his chair, and hastily turned up Barbary.

"Here it is. 'Barbary, Sir Theodore, of Easterbrook. Created 1590, son of Bertram Barbary, born 27 Jan. 1830, s. 1870.' What does 's' stand for, I wonder?"

"Succeeded, I should think. That's when Sir Walter died, isn't it?"

"'Succeeded 1870, married Aline, daughter of W. S. Clements of Detroit, one son, two daughters. Present address Detroit, United States of America. Heir, Eugene, born 4 Mar. 1861.'" Thomas turned the book over. "1885. There was still an heir then."

"I wonder why they left Easterbrook?"

"And who was Bertram Barbary? I didn't find him in the churchyard this morning."

"This must be the cousin the Misses Siskin told me about."

"I should have thought he would have come back to Easterbrook, not sold it," said Thomas slowly. "Perhaps a cousin would not want to. A brother would have done."

There was a pause, and then Dora voiced the thought in both their minds.

"Not if he knew about the body."

Four

FRIDAY was the day when the gentle routine of Easterbrook was altered to include an excursion to the county town of Calleford. Thomas still could not get used to the idea that this bustling market town, with its twin-towered Minster, was a real city within the meaning of the word. It might well be the commercial, social and religious centre of the county of Calleshire, Easterbrook included, but it didn't rank as a city with him. He had his own ideas of what constituted a metropolis.

Friday was also the day when the Calleford weekly newspaper appeared. Thomas and Dora were still at breakfast and deep in newspapers written and printed in London when Gladys appeared and said, "Hasn't Mr. Harding come out well?"

Thomas, who could not think what it was she was talking about, hid behind his paper, while Dora, more practically, asked her.

"*The Courier.* Haven't you seen it? Mr. Harding's on the front page."

The Courier had done the skeleton well. Thomas, the Manor, the skeleton and the inquest occupied the two right-hand columns of the front page. The two left-hand columns were devoted to the murder of someone called the Calleford blonde. There was a photograph of Thomas taken leaving the Guildhall. There was also a studio photograph of the Calleford blonde—taken well before the murder.

"Not bad," said Thomas. It was impossible to tell which photograph he was looking at. "Not bad at all," he added enigmatically.

At the end of the story about the skeleton there was a

photograph of the Manor. The whole report was dignified and restrained. Much to Thomas's surprise the same could be said for the story about the Calleford blonde. *The Courier* gave the impression that it was reporting the murder only because it happened in Calleford. It was its duty to report what happened in Calleford, and report it it would; but it would not enjoy murder. It would not gloat over it. The paper Thomas had been reading, national in circulation if not in stature, showed no such reservations. It was positively wallowing in the Calleford blonde in striking (and ungrammatical) headlines and tear-jerking paragraphs.

Usually on Fridays Thomas would shop for his own simple wants in Calleford and then repair to the lounge of The Tabard where presently Dora would join him for luncheon. This modest programme worked very well as a rule, and they were able to drive back to Easterbrook in the early afternoon with the week's shopping in the car, conscious of having had a mild outing.

This Friday Thomas left his devoted wife outside Calleford's largest haberdashers and went off in search of the public library. He had had an idea, one which he hadn't even mentioned to Dora in case it led up a blind alley. It had come to him after reading the little Baronet-age the Misses Siskin had lent them. If there had been a Barbary alive with an heir in 1885 then it was just possible that that heir had a son and a grandson, and if he were still alive then the Barbary family would still be in the Baronetage.

The policeman on duty at the pedestrian crossing directed him.

"You can't miss the library, sir. A new building with two of them modern statues outside. The Rose and the Crown we call 'em."

Thomas looked curiously about him. It was a new building, and in a place like Calleford, that alone made it conspicuous. And if the building were not new enough it was fronted by two sculptures so abstract as to be ludicrous. He stared at them unbelievingly. If one had not had "Literature" engraved on its plinth and the other "Art" he would have thought someone had played a trick on the

Corporation. As it was, he still wasn't quite sure that they
hadn't. "Literature" had a crown of laurels on its head,
while "Art" was considering a rose and her expression was
ambiguous indeed. So they had come to be known as the
Rose and Crown. How very, very English. In other countries they might have been tarred and feathered, or
painted red, or blown up, or taken down, or—worst of
all—considered Great Works of Art. But not in Calleford,
England. They had just been amiably and aptly re-
christened and that was that. Gentle ridicule would keep
them in their proper place.

Unconsciously Thomas had quickened his pace as he
neared the building, and he found himself standing
breathless at the top of the library steps. Fortunately the
reference library was on the ground floor and he made his
way there more slowly. Lugging down the heavy Baronetage from a high shelf and carrying it across to a table
brought on another attack of breathlessness, but his effort
was well rewarded.

There was a Barbary of Easterbrook listed.

This was a much more detailed affair than the other
Baronetage. It began with the creation of the first Sir
Tobias in 1590, and worked its way slowly and carefully
through the fifteen holders of the title to the present day.
There was a Sir Thaddeus Barbary still living in Detroit,
U.S.A., but Thomas wasn't interested in him. It was the
sixth, seventh, eighth and ninth baronets he was after. It
wasn't easy to find them among the small print and
abbreviations, but at last he put a finger against the sixth
Sir Toby who died in 1748. Thomas knew that already
from the gravestone.

He was succeeded by his son, the 7th Baronet, who
died in 1799 having issue. Thomas looked closely at the
page—this was interesting. "Having issue, 1. Toby, 8th
Bart, b. 1775, s. 1799, m. Fanny, d. of William Marden,
gentleman, of Maplegate, d.s.p.s. 1815. One s. Toby
d.v.p. 2. Richard, 9th Bart, b. 1778..."

Thomas felt his pulse quicken. Toby, the 8th Baronet
had had a son then even though he had been succeeded
by his brother. Dora had been right. It *was* odd that there
should have been a change of Christian name. Hastily he

turned over the pages of the heavy volume. If those abbreviations meant what he thought they did he was on to something. He ran his finger down the page.

"d.s.p.s. decessit sine prole superstite."

"d.v.p. decessit vita patris."

Thomas knew no Latin and he was about to carry the Baronetage bodily in search of someone who did when he spotted an English translation.

"d.s.p.s. died without surviving issue."

"d.v.p. died in the lifetime of the father."

"I knew it," he said aloud.

An elderly lady in the reference library looked up disapprovingly. Thomas was unabashed. He was sure he had found out who his skeleton was; moreover the elderly lady looked as if she was using the reference library solely for solving a crossword in a literary weekly. His business here was more important than that. He jotted down a few notes and hurried out of the library with barely a sideways glance at the Rose and Crown.

He was impatient for the arrival of Dora at The Tabard, but when she came he said nothing of his researches. They went through into the dining-room to their usual table and were seated before Dora noticed a half bottle of red wine on the table. She looked at him enquiringly.

"Thomas, I do believe you've discovered something."

His face creased into a broad smile. He had been married to her for nearly thirty years and had never ceased to marvel at her womanly perception. They had never had children but that was all their marriage lacked.

"I think I have, my dear."

"Not—not who he was?"

"I think he was the son of the eighth Sir Toby who was killed at Waterloo. He had a son who died in his father's lifetime. That was how the name changed. A brother inherited instead."

"What was the boy called?"

"Toby—like his father."

"He was the last Toby in the family then?"

"Well, I hadn't thought of it like that, but I suppose he was."

"Can you be sure—I mean absolutely sure?"

Thomas considered this. "Probably not yet. It's just a strong possibility—let's say a probability—at the moment. What I will have to do is to have another look round that churchyard and in the church. There may be a grave there of this son which I missed the other day. He might even have been an infant—don't forget the baronetage doesn't say how old he was. I'll do that this afternoon."

"Tomorrow," said his wife firmly.

But in Easterbrook churchyard there was no grave of a Toby Barbary who had died in his father's lifetime. Thomas spent the whole Saturday morning there—much to the amusement of the choirboys who were having their practice. They were so curious that in the end he enlisted their aid. They, too, found all the other Barbary memorials including those of the good Sir Richard and the gallant Sir Toby who was killed at Waterloo. But no Toby who died between 1775 and 1815. Thomas found himself explaining his quest, a little defensively perhaps, to the choirmaster and organist, Cousens.

"Even if he's not here in the churchyard I can't be sure that he would be my skeleton because I don't know how old he was when he died. The skeleton was about fifteen or sixteen."

"You want the Parish Registers," said the organist, tucking a stray sheet of music under his arm.

"The Parish Registers?" echoed Thomas.

"Yes, the Rector's got them. You could find out when this Toby of yours was born, couldn't you? That would help, and if he died and was buried in the parish that would be in them too."

"Would it now?" said Thomas thoughtfully. "I'll do that."

"Come on, boys," Cousens called loudly, and then in a bitter aside to Thomas, "I'd no idea they could be a nuisance when they were dead as well."

Thomas laughed at his cynicism and went home to suggest that Mr. Martindale be invited to dinner. Dora countered this with the suggestion that they went to church next day and asked him then. Thomas acquiesced, and Sunday morning found them both in the pew under the memorial to Sir Richard Barbary of Easterbrook, Benefactor of this Parish. Not far away on a pillar was a

memorial to Sir Toby Barbary of Easterbrook, Justice of
the Peace, Colonel of the 123rd The Calleshire Regiment,
who fell at the Battle of Waterloo, "erected by his
sorrowing wife and brother officers as a token of the high
esteem in which they held him".

"Do you think the firm will do that for me?" whispered
Thomas during the First Lesson.

Dora favoured him with a repressive look and hoped he
wouldn't get restive during the sermon.

"Where is the sorrowing wife, anyway?" he sang in her
ear while everyone else was singing "Dear Lord and
Father of Mankind".

"Perhaps she's in the churchyard," hissed Dora out of
the corner of her mouth. "Women didn't count as much
then, did they?"

"I don't remember seeing her there. She should be in
here with her husband," sang Thomas severely. He took
out his notebook and scribbled something in it until his
eye was caught by an outraged churchwarden.

The evening the Rector spent with them was pure joy.
Thomas had had little contact with the Church in his
lifetime, and that mostly with muscular and/or militant
clergy in slum parishes, so he was ill-prepared for the
Reverend Cyprian Martindale. He was older, much older
than Thomas had realised, and very gracious. After the
meal they went through into the drawing-room. Thomas
pushed aside the panel to show him the secret room.

"A priest's hole beyond a doubt, Mr. Harding. This was
built for a recusant priest, though one cannot tell whether
one ever lived in it. The only people who might be able to
help you would be the Catholic Record Society."

"But you said the Barbarys weren't Catholics."

The rector inclined his head. "They could have
renounced their faith and become Protestant—those were
hard times for Catholics you know. Or the family which
built the house could have been fined so heavily for not
going to church that they had to sell their house."

"And that was where the Barbarys came in?"

"They may well have done. As I said, times were hard
for Catholics but they were also good times for some
people. It was not uncommon for a Catholic family to be

reduced to great poverty—as it was not unknown for a good Elizabethan man of business to set himself up for life, buy a house like this—and collect a title into the bargain."

Thomas sat down and observed diffidently that there were worse ambitions.

The clergyman looked round the drawing-room.

"Many, many more, Mr. Harding. If I may say so, I think the ownership and preservation of a room like this is a most worthy ambition."

"You know this may sound very naïve to you, Rector, but I hope that first Sir Tobias Barbary *was* an Elizabethan adventurer. I shall feel more at home here now. He would have felt very much as I do, making his pile and coming to live in somebody else's house. If it's as you say, he would have been *nouveau riche* in his time too."

Mr. Martindale demurred at this, but Thomas was firm.

"Times have been good for me, too, Rector. It's a happy thought that I might have something in common with that first Sir Tobias. I shan't feel so badly about living in his house now." He made as if to attend to the fire. "I feel Easterbrook thinks of us as usurpers at times."

The clergyman smiled. "Let us say rather that we are all in our time inheritors of what has gone before. You, I think, have inherited an unusual legacy from the past."

"The skeleton? Yes, it's not everyone who has a ready-made puzzle in their own drawing-room."

Dora entered with coffee.

"Your husband has been showing me your secret room, Mrs. Harding," said the Rector.

"Has he?" remarked Dora drily.

"I've found out quite a bit about the skeleton, you know," said Thomas hastily, "as well as what the pathologist told us." He reached for the notebook which nowadays was seldom far from his side. "Did you know that the eighth Sir Toby Barbary had a son who died in his father's lifetime?"

The Rector nodded.

"You did!" Thomas's disappointment was patent.

"You forget, Mr. Harding, that I have a choir full of boys. They may sing like angels, some of them indeed look like angels but they are not angels. They spent all of Saturday afternoon looking for your Toby Barbary. They even cleaned up the unreadable tombstones—a labour for which the church normally pays a great deal."

Thomas hung his head. "I fear I did—er—hint at largesse."

"You aroused their interest," said Mr. Martindale kindly.

"Of course, the fact that he is not in the churchyard is not conclusive. He could be buried somewhere else, he could have been an infant without a gravestone—or he could have been put in this room. All I am sure of is that he died before Waterloo. I don't even know when he was born."

Mr. Martindale accepted a cup of coffee. "I can't help you there—but I can tell you that he was baptised on February 1st, 1800."

"You can?" said Thomas eagerly. "How do you know?"

"You forget, Mr. Harding, that I have an organist as well as a choir. It occurred to me tonight you might be interested in having the information tonight." He reached into his pocket while Thomas and Dora avoided each other's eye. "I've got it written down somewhere. Ah, here we are. On February 1st, 1800, a son of Sir Toby Barbary of Easterbrook and Fanny, his wife, was baptised Toby by the incumbent of the time and the fact duly noted in the Parish Register."

"Did he die?" said Thomas urgently.

Mr. Martindale smiled. "Well, not in this parish according to the registers. I looked through them right up to 1815 when his father was killed."

"How very kind," interjected Dora.

The Rector set down his cup. "It is very right and proper that your husband should wish to see justice done."

Thomas looked uncomfortable and hurriedly consulted his notebook.

"Don't you think it odd that I can't find him in the churchyard? We know for certain he was dead before Waterloo else he would have been the 9th Baronet."

"He could have died away somewhere."

"Possibly, but look at it this way: we know there was a son of this house born around 1800 who died before 1815 but who was not buried here in his own parish. And in this house I found a skeleton of a boy of about fifteen who died about a hundred and fifty years ago. If that's coincidence I'll eat my hat."

The clergyman shook his head. "No, that's not coincidence, Mr. Harding. I'm not a lawyer but I'd say you had everything except proof."

"It may be where I come to a full stop, of course," admitted Thomas, "but there are still some things I don't understand—particularly how it was that Charlie Ford's grandfather knew about that secret room."

"That certainly requires an explanation."

"And Toby's mother, Rector. My husband noticed she wasn't in the churchyard—nor in the church either."

"Now, let me see, who exactly was she?"

"One Fanny Marden of Staplegate."

"Ah, yes. Now that's about fifteen miles from here. Why isn't she there, I wonder?"

"I don't know." Thomas snapped his notebook shut. "I don't even know where to go from here."

The Rector thought for a moment or two and then said, "You could try *The Courier* of course."

"The paper you mean? Would they know anything?"

"It's a pretty old-established affair. They just might have an obituary of the chap who was killed at Waterloo. He would have been quite a well-known person round here in his own day. What do the police say?"

"The police are more interested in their other body," said Thomas a trifle bitterly. "The Calleford blonde."

"Ah, yes," said Mr. Martindale surprisingly. "Mary Fenny. She was strangled you know, manually. A very nasty business. The husband has disappeared, so naturally the police suspect him." He sighed gently. "I suppose one mustn't blame them for that." He caught sight of Dora's face. "I surprise you, Mrs. Harding?"

Dora looked quite confused. "I didn't think . . . the details of murder . . ." her voice tailed off.

"Should be the concern of the clergy?" he finished the sentence for her. "On the contrary murder is evil and evil should always be the concern of the Church. I am deeply concerned about the death of Mary Fenny."

"You knew her then," said Dora gently.

"Indeed, I did. Her parents live in Easterbrook, you know. I baptised her here, and married her too. She even taught in the Sunday School for a while."

"I'd never have thought it," said Dora involuntarily. "To read the newspapers one would never have thought—well—that she was that sort of a girl."

"I think sometimes that the Press, too, should be the concern of the Church," said the Rector. "In its way it can do as much harm as murder."

"She must have been very good looking," said Thomas. "There was nothing wrong with the photograph in *The Courier*."

"She was indeed. Everyone considered Alan Fenny was a lucky lad. And now the police think he killed her."

"Do you?" asked Dora directly.

Mr. Martindale gave the sigh of an old man. "She was very beautiful," was all he would say.

Thomas took the Rector's advice and sought out the offices of the Calleford *Courier*. They were near the public library, and he paused on the pavement for a moment to look at the twin statues, the Rose and Crown. Their enormity struck him afresh. He had almost decided that "Literature" was the more outrageous—until he had another look at "Art". After the modern sculpture, *The Courier* offices were refreshingly conventional. He explained his errand to an elderly clerk.

"Waterloo? *The Courier* wouldn't have covered the battle, you know. Just a short report I expect."

"It's not the battle I'm interested in," said Thomas, "but an obituary of someone who was killed at it."

"Ah, that's different." The clerk smiled confidently. "*The Courier* would publish an obituary of anyone local. Will you come this way?"

He led Thomas through the outer office and down a steep flight of stairs into a large basement. It was lined with large bound volumes of *The Courier*. They were all in red leather and had just the year printed on their spines. The clerk lifted down the one marked 1815 and left Thomas to his researches.

He turned over the thin yellowed pages carefully until he came to June. The clerk had been right. There was just a short note announcing that intelligence had been received of a victory of the army under the Duke of Wellington at a place called Waterloo. There was no mention of Sir Toby Barbary in that issue. Thomas went on turning the pages. The paper of the next week carried a brief list of officers of the Calleshire Regiment who were known to have fallen in battle. It was in the issue of the week after that that Thomas found what he was looking for.

The Courier had done full justice to the memory of that very gallant English officer and gentleman, Colonel Sir Toby Barbary of Easterbrook, Colonel of the Calleshire Regiment, Justice of the Peace. It paid tribute to his services to his regiment in war and peace, including his willingness to make the ultimate sacrifice of laying down his life for King and Country. It recalled his services to the county, called him a widely respected figure throughout the neighbourhood, pointed out how genuinely he would be mourned, and regretted that so able a man should be cut off in his prime.

The Courier extended its sympathies to the colonel's widow, a member of a family well known in another part of the county, a daughter of Mr. William Marden of Staplegate. ("Fifteen miles would be quite a distance then," agreed Thomas). *The Courier* observed that the colonel's death in battle was particularly distressing for his family, coming, as it did, so soon after the tragic death of his only son.

Thomas felt his heart throbbing uncomfortably. The booklined basement was so silent that its beat seemed to him to be audible. He lifted his head from the paper. It was quite ridiculous that he, a hard-headed man of business, should be disturbed by a hundred-and-fifty-year-old newspaper report. After a moment or two his pulse steadied again and he bent over the obituary.

There was very little more. Just a brief statement that the new baronet was Sir Richard Barbary, Sir Toby's younger brother.

Five

THOMAS reached for his notebook; but he needed nothing to refresh his memory. He knew Toby Barbary was born around 1800 and now he knew he died "tragically" just before his father was killed in 1815. And he, Thomas, had found the skeleton of a fifteen-year-old boy in that same Toby's ancestral home.

He turned back the old pages impatiently. This was no coincidence. Now to find a report of the death of the boy. *The Courier* wouldn't have missed that.

The Courier hadn't missed it, in fact the story took second place only to a report of the theft of a chalice from Calleford Minster. Thomas found it in a copy of the newspaper dated a few weeks before Waterloo. "Tragic Disappearance of Baronet's Son", ran the heading. "Melancholy Event at Easterbrook", said the sub-title. Thomas bent eagerly over the smaller print.

Young Toby Barbary, it seemed, had disappeared one fine afternoon in early May, the day of the Easterbrook Fair. One Giles Shambrook had seen him fishing from the river bank about three o'clock in the afternoon, had lifted his cap to the squire's young son and gone on his way. When the boy had not returned to the Manor by evening a search had been organised and the boy's uncle, Mr. Richard Barbary, had found his fishing rod tangled in some over-hanging bushes. Next day the boy's shoe had been hooked up from some river weeds not far from the spot where the fishing rod had been found. The river had been searched as far as was practicable but, as *The Courier* reminded its readers, the river Calle ran deep and swift through Easterbook and especially at the point above the bridge where the fishing rod had been found.

The Courier deeply sympathized with all the young man's relatives at such a tragic event, especially as it had occurred during his father's absence with the Duke of Wellington's forces. Though only young, Master Toby had endeared himself to all and sundry as an upright, God-fearing youth, a worthy son of a much-respected father.

In spite of a notice imploring him to handle the old volumes with care Thomas practically slammed the bound newspapers shut.

"Drowned my foot," he said to Dora half an hour later across the luncheon table at The Tabard. He regarded the pages of his notebook with disfavour. "The whole story stinks. That lad wasn't drowned. He was hit on the head—hard, and then bundled into that secret room." He glared ferociously at an innocent, if inattentive, waiter.

"Poor boy," said Dora. "So our skeleton really is Toby Barbary."

"I'm certain of it. He was murdered as surely as that girl Mary Fenny was murdered. And whoever planted that fishing rod on the river bank had a hand in it."

"Chicken or fish, dear?"

"And that shoe must have been thrown in, too. What was that?"

"The menu. Chicken or fish?"

"Fish please—no, I'll have chicken. Look here, Dora, I'm going to get to the bottom of this somehow."

"Someone must have murdered him," agreed Dora pensively. "But there must have been a reason. Why do people murder other people?"

"There's anger," said Thomas. "You know—that 'blind rage' sort."

"And religion."

"Yes, and—what's it called these days?—status saving."

"Pride is what that's called," said Dora crisply. "And then there's murder to get a legal heir."

Thomas paused for a moment. "Henry the Eighth. I hadn't thought of that."

"I'm delighted to hear it."

Thomas grinned and kept silent.

"That just leaves us with the two commonest reasons," said Dora practically.

"Love?"

"Passion," said his wife. "Jealousy. The Calleford blonde sort of murder."

"And gain."

"It's not often anyone benefits from the death of a child."

"There's inheritance—a sub-division of gain. That would be the uncle, I suppose." Thomas turned over his portion of chicken and considered Toby Barbary's uncle. "Isn't that the public benefactor one?"

"The ninth baronet," agreed Dora, "but it couldn't be him. He can't have known that his brother was going to be killed a few weeks later."

Thomas nodded. "Murdering your own nephew isn't entirely consistent with public benefaction."

And so, for the second Saturday running, Thomas spent the morning in the churchyard. His aim was to get into the church but he could hear the choir practising still. He went not to the Barbary graves but to the newer, tidier part of the churchyard. There he soon found "Matilda Meredith of Easterbrook Manor", who died in 1941, aged 79. She hadn't known the secret of the Manor, but not far away was the grave of one who had. Thomas came to a halt before some plain white marble on which was written simply "Obadiah Ford, born 12 March 1859, died 27 October 1942, aged 83," and later, in slightly different lettering, "and Eliza, widow of the above, died 1 September 1943, aged 82."

He was still looking at this stone when the choirboys came clattering out of the church. Obadiah Ford had known something all right. Thomas grinned ruefully at the white marble. Cliché or not, the old chap had taken his secret to the grave. The choirboys streamed down the churchyard paths, precariously freewheeling their bicycles where they were forbidden to ride them, and Thomas made his way into the church.

The organist, Cousens, was playing to himself and the little church was filled with a chorale fit for a cathedral. He saw Thomas and finished with a massive chord.

"There's nothing quite like it," he said obliquely.

"Satisfying," agreed Thomas.

"It's a new organ, of course," said Cousens, "but then I dare say you know that."

Thomas, whose subscription had headed the list, nodded.

"It's not bad, not bad at all," said Cousens, "and they even made quite a good job of fitting it inside the old case . . ."

Thomas feigned a polite interest and was led off to inspect it. Then suddenly his interest ceased to be polite and became genuine. Set in the old organ case was a little brass plate declaring it to be the gift to the church in 1830 of Sir Richard Barbary. He peered forward.

"Ah, yes," said Cousens. "You're interested in the family, aren't you? Did you ever find that boy you were looking for?"

"In a way," said Thomas slowly, "but Sir Richard interests me too. I've come to have a look at him in here."

Cousens walked down the chancel with him to the Manor House pew. On the wall above it was the memorial to Sir Richard Barbary of Easterbrook, 9th Baronet, benefactor of this parish.

"There's more about him in the tower," said Cousens. He pointed to some heavy red curtains hanging at the end of the main aisle. "You'll find all you want there."

Thomas thanked him and pushed the curtains aside. He found himself standing at the base of a square tower among empty flower vases, dusters, and a row of cassocks hanging limply on pegs. On a little table a box full of hymn numbers had spilled out. On the walls above were hanging wooden boards.

The writing on them was old and faded, and the wood dark and in shadow, but Thomas persisted in his efforts to read what was written. Somewhere must lie a clue to the murderer of young Toby Barbary.

"Sir Richard Barbary gave on January 1st, 1816, the sum of £500 unto the Minister and Churchwardens of this Parish for the time being, to be by them Invested in the Public Funds of Great Britain, the proceeds thereof to be devoted to the maintenance of homes for Three deserving Poor Men and Three deserving Poor Women, who shall belong to or have resided in the Parish for one Twelve-month at the least."

The second board was in rather better light.

"Sir Richard Barbary gave on March 1st, 1816, the sum of £200 to be invested by the Minister and Churchwardens of this Parish for the time being in one or more of the Parliamentary Stocks and the interest thereof to be equally divided at the discretion of the said Minister and Churchwardens between Six deserving Poor Men, who shall be more than Fifty years of age and who shall belong to or have resided in the Parish for one Twelvemonth at the least immediately preceding the day of distribution."

He further directed that this Charity should be distributed "on or before Maundy Thursday in every year."

Thomas faithfully copied these benefactions into his notebook. Sir Richard had been generous indeed to his native parish. Five hundred pounds was a good endowment for almshouses in 1816 even if invested in the Public Funds of Great Britain. He had no great affection for Government Stock himself and wondered what sort of interest the money was earning now. Automatically he did a few quick calculations in the margin of his notebook—and then scribbled through them ruefully when he remembered how out of touch he was with the money market.

Thomas heard footsteps in the aisle and decided that if the organist were going now, he too would be on his way. He closed his notebook and slipped out between the curtains. But it wasn't Cousens the organist with whom he came face to face. Walking towards him was a younger man, untidy and hurried. He stopped abruptly when he saw Thomas.

Thomas stopped too and nodded in a friendly way. "I thought you must be the organist," he said. "He was here earlier."

"He left five minutes ago." The young man was a little out of breath. His voice uneducated but pleasant. His clothes though were very much the worse for wear. "I was—er—in the churchyard. I didn't think there would be anyone here. Mr. Cousens always stays on after choir practice to play a little while on his own. I didn't think there would be anyone here now," he repeated.

"Well, I'm just going so there won't be in a moment," said Thomas comfortably. "I just came to look up the Barbary Charities. They're in the bell tower, you know."

"Yes, I know." The young man gave a short laugh. "Believe it or not, I used to be in the choir. That's how I knew about Mr. Cousens staying on on Saturdays. I could tell you what those boards say word for word I've read them so often."

Thomas smiled. "You'll have to wait until you're fifty to get much help from the Barbary Charities I'm afraid."

The man regarded him with a curious expression on his face. "I don't want charity. I want sanctuary."

"Then I hope you may find it here," said Thomas simply, turning to go. As he opened the church door he saw the man sink into a pew and bury his face in his hands.

He reported on his morning's researches to Dora at lunchtime.

"I think we may be able to rule out Sir Richard as our murderer—there's no doubt about the Barbary benefactions. He did give a lot of money to the parish in the two Charities mentioned in the church alone." Thomas sunk his knife into an excellent steak. "You'll be glad to know that when I've lived here twelve months I shall be eligible for a place in an almshouse."

"I hope the food will be good," observed Dora piously.

"It's a very good steak anyway," he said defensively. "Do you know where the almshouses are, by the way?"

"Down by the river, I think. There's a row of tiny cottages there, all exactly alike. They look quite pretty from the outside but I expect they're uncivilised enough if we only knew. Six of them, I think."

"That's right. Three deserving Poor Men and Three deserving Poor Women."

"I don't think you'd like it."

"Are they still inhabited? I can't remember ever noticing."

Dora nodded. "Yes, I know they are, because Gladys was telling me that Mrs. Fenny lives there."

"Mrs. Fenny—but I thought she'd been murdered?"

"Her mother-in-law. Apparently her landlord put her out soon after her son Alan married Mary, and the Rector let her have one of the almshouses. She's been a widow for years."

"And Mary Fenny's people still live in Easterbrook too?"

Dora nodded again. "In the High Street. They're better off than Mrs. Fenny but Alan got himself a good job and they agreed to the wedding all right."

There was a silence and then she said suddenly, "Thomas, Gladys was telling me all about her. She was a nice girl, you know. And so was her husband. Gladys is quite firm about that. No one in Easterbrook thinks he did it. They were so much in love." Dora's kind face was distressed.

"If he didn't, why has he disappeared?" said Thomas soberly. "It's not a sign of innocence as a rule."

"Perhaps he was frightened," suggested Dora. "He came back and found her, you know."

"I thought the milkman found her."

"So did everyone else at first, but the police found Alan Fenny's fingerprints on a tumbler by her bed."

"They *were* husband and wife."

"Ah, but he hadn't been home that night. They'd had a quarrel, you see, and the fingerprints were on top of Mary Fenny's."

"Only he could have put them there," pointed out Thomas reasonably.

"But he didn't do it," persisted Dora. "Everyone is sure about that."

"The evidence isn't in his favour, is it? A history of a quarrel, fingerprint proof that he was in the room that night, and then his complete disappearance. The police will pick him up sooner or later, you'll see," said Thomas confidently. "And they'll sort it out. Innocent men don't go to prison in England, you know."

Dora looked unconvinced.

"They don't you know. You wait and see. The police are bound to catch him, and if he didn't do it, they'll catch the real murderer." Thomas smiled faintly. "This is the middle of the twentieth century, not the early nineteenth. The police may not care who murdered Toby Barbary but you'll find they care quite a bit about who strangled Mary Fenny."

Thomas did not sleep well that night. And at two o'clock in the morning he woke from an involved dream in which both Toby Barbary and Mary Fenny seemed to be trying to tell him something. He had never seen either of them alive, but in the curious manner of dreams this did not seem to matter.

He woke suddenly, painfully conscious of the wayward thuds of his heart. For a moment he thought he heard some other sound as well and he turned to look at his wife. Dora, however, was sleeping soundly by his side, and so he lay there in the darkness patiently waiting for his heartbeat to return to normal, and for sleep to overtake him. Capriciously, and just because he wanted it so, it would not come. Instead, as the slow minutes went by he became increasingly wakeful.

He turned his mind back to his dream. Who had murdered Toby Barbary? What manner of man could crush the skull of a fifteen-year-old boy? And what possible motive could that man have had?

A moment later Thomas stiffened. He hadn't been mistaken then. There had been an alien sound in the house and it had just been repeated. It wasn't a bad dream which had woken him after all.

He slipped out of bed. He saw no point in waking Dora, who would only be alarmed, and as like as not forbid him the excitement of routing a burglar.

His foot was on the top stair when he heard another sound. It came from the drawing-room. Gingerly he descended another step. The staircase was broad and shallow after the fashion of old houses, and bare of carpeting. Going down it noiselessly wasn't easy, but by the time he reached the bottom Thomas was almost enjoying himself. He wasn't particularly worried about what a burglar might steal. He had not made his money easily enough to spend it on *objets d'art* which he neither understood nor appreciated, and such possessions as he had were well insured. He tightened his lips ironically. Perhaps it was as well that Dora's weakness had always been for hats rather than silver.

Once in the hall he groped his way to the front door where his heavy walking stick always stood. Thus armed he approached the drawing-room, and in one swift movement threw open the door and turned on the electric light.

There was nobody there.

Thomas clutched his walking stick firmly and stepped into the room. There was still nothing to see. He prodded the curtains with his stick and poked it behind chairs without finding anything. He even peered up the old Elizabethan chimney in case the thief had gone that way.

"That's odd," he murmured half aloud. "I could have sworn—" and then he nearly jumped out of his skin as something touched the back of his leg. He looked down and laughed in amusement and relief.

"Sammy, you silly cat. What are you doing in here?"

The big marmalade cat rubbed himself against Thomas's pyjama trousers, purring away. He stooped to stroke him.

"You should be outside keeping the mice down instead of waking me up. I thought you were a burglar. Come along."

Thomas led the way to the front door, gently drew back the bolts and tipped the cat outside. He replaced his walking stick with a smile at his own stupidity and began to climb the stairs back to bed.

He stopped abruptly on the eighth step.

He had put Sammy outside himself at eleven o'clock. Thomas turned round and descended the stairs, thinking carefully. Dora had gone to bed at half past ten, and he had locked up and put Sammy out about half an hour later. He put the hall light on, and went carefully round the ground floor checking the doors and windows. Perhaps he had missed a window last night. But he hadn't. They were all as firmly shut as he had left them at eleven o'clock. The doors, too, were locked and bolted, save for the back one which was latched and for which Gladys had a key. Thomas and Dora, being town people, began their day a good two hours after everyone else in Easterbrook, and providing Gladys with her own key had averted any crises arising out of this.

Thomas stood in the hall and wondered. Sammy, whom

he had put out at eleven, had most definitely been back in again at two o'clock. And there were no open windows through which he could have climbed in. Sammy was a big cat though, and could easily have accounted for the noise which had woken Thomas, especially if he had been locked in a room when he would rather have been outside.

He stopped again. Locked in? The drawing-room door had been shut when Thomas came down. Had the cat come down the chimney then? He shrugged his shoulders. He was beginning to be tired now. He would investigate the chimney in the morning. They used to put children up them, didn't they? He reckoned that Sammy could go anywhere a child could go.

He climbed quietly back into bed and was almost asleep when logic tossed him a thought.

"No cat, not even Sammy, could climb *down* a chimney in the dark. Up, perhaps, but not down. Anyway he would have to get on the roof first."

"He must have got in there somehow," argued Thomas's other self.

"All the windows were shut," responded logic smartly. "You've just checked."

"I'll think about it in the morning," he temporized.

"It'll need a lot of thought."

"In the morning," he pleaded. "I'm very tired."

Six

GLADYS did not work at the Manor on Sundays, and as a consequence of this and his disturbed night Thomas overslept. This meant he had barely time to get to church for Matins, certainly none to spare in which to tell Dora about the mysterious re-entry of Sammy. He wasn't absolutely sure that he wanted to tell Dora about it anyway, not until he had had a chance to think about it himself.

He had mentally reserved sermon time for a spot of quiet thinking on the problem, but when the Rector mounted the pulpit steps and gave out his text Thomas's attention was caught by both the man and what he had to say. The clergyman looked older than ever as he climbed slowly up to the pulpit and surveyed his congregation, but his voice was clear.

"The Bible says: 'Render therefore unto Caesar the things which are Caesar's.' It is a quotation which we all know but one which we don't use very often, except perhaps when we pay our income tax. Yet it means far more than a monetary tribute to a government. It means agreeing to and conforming with a rule of civil law."

He leaned over the edge of the pulpit and repeated the last sentence. "It means agreeing to and conforming with a rule of civil law. In England we have a happy tradition of agreeing amongst ourselves on the constitution of that civil law, which is in itself a good reason for obeying it."

He set his thumbs in the folds of his cassock.

"There are always those who will split hairs over the differences between sin and crime. That is no refuge today. There are always those who will disregard the laws of State while maintaining they have not offended God. My people, it is rarely possible to oppose civil law

57

without harming one's fellow-citizens. Certainly not in this case. You don't need me to tell you that harming your fellow-citizens is in its way equally an offence against God."

Thomas sat up, all attention. What law was being broken so flagrantly in Easterbrook that the Rector could denounce it from the pulpit? The old voice went on purposefully.

"But you do need me to tell you that the ends of justice must be served and in a lawful manner. My friends, I have lived among you for many, many years and few of you have not complained to me at some time or other of the injustice of life. None of you has ever complained to me of the injustice of the law. It is that civil law which we normally so much respect that must now be allowed to take its course."

The Rector had no notes and now he leaned over his pulpit and looked directly at his congregation. Thomas stirred uneasily in his hard pew, genuinely glad of a clear conscience. He wouldn't have liked to have to meet those honest old eyes without it. Something in that pregnant silence seemed to reach the man in the pulpit, for when he spoke again his voice was full of compassion.

"Do not think that I do not understand your feelings. I, too, feel deeply." Here for the first time his voice shook a little. "Very deeply indeed but the ends of justice must be served. We all come before the Great Judge in the end, where, alas, we shall only get what we deserve, but the innocent have little to fear from Caesar's judge in England today. I say unto you that which is Caesar's must be rendered unto Caesar. And now to God, the Father..."

The Rector was one of those clergymen who usually stood by the church door after a service, shaking hands with his congregation as they filed out. Thomas had been looking forward to murmuring to him that he had identified his skeleton and inviting him to the Manor to hear all about it. But after the choir had wended their way to the bell tower the Rector disappeared into his vestry.

The congregation waited for him for a few moments and then Cousens, the organist, began to play the voluntary. Gradually people took the hint and began to leave the

hurch without their customary chat with Mr. Martindale.
Thomas remained puzzled and said so to Dora as they
ambled slowly up the church path.

"Perhaps Gladys knows what the sermon is all about,"
he suggested.

"That's another thing," said Thomas. "She wasn't in
church. It's the first time I've known her not be there."

"How do you know?" Dora was amused and curious.
"She sits a long way behind our pew and you didn't look
round."

"Our Gladys's singing voice is quite inimitable,"
retorted her husband feelingly. "You can take it from me
he wasn't there. We were all in tune this morning."

"I think one of us must be out of step," murmured
Dora, "if that sermon meant anything at all."

"It meant something all right," averred Thomas, "but I
don't know what."

They threaded their way through the congregation
which was now spread out along the path. They received
the odd greeting as they passed, but it was obvious that
Thomas and Dora were strangers. They were both aware
of a peculiar atmosphere this morning and an unusual
silence hung over the usually chatty scene. Thomas and
Dora hurried on their way.

"I shall be quite glad to get back home," said Dora,
shivering a little. "Easterbrook isn't its usual self today."

Thomas agreed and set his key into the lock of the front
door. Sammy, the cat, walked across the hall to greet
them.

"That's funny," said Dora. "I thought I put him out
before we went to church. Did you let him in again?"

"I must have done," said Thomas quickly; but he hadn't.
In fact he distinctly remembered seeing the cat in the
garden as they walked to church.

His afternoon rest was one of the things Thomas most
resented about his illness. It was anathema to him to be
lying down at two o'clock in the afternoon. All his working
life he had waged an unrelenting war on protracted business luncheons. Anyone who worked for Thomas had had
to be back at his desk by 2:15 and always found Thomas
there before him. To find himself actually lying down

every afternoon seemed to him the ultimate indignity. At first he had protested, but he was powerless against the combination of his helpmeet and his medical adviser. Dr Curzan strongly recommended and Dora stringently enforced a routine guaranteed to suit his heart, not the working habits of a lifetime.

This afternoon, however, Thomas made for his bedroom without demur. He had a fine choice of subjects on which to ponder.

He was now as certain as he could be that the skeleton was that of young Toby Barbary who hadn't ended up in the river after all but in the secret room. His uncle who succeeded must be the first suspect—however unlikely he seemed as a murderer; but there must be other suspects too . . .

Then there was the rector's sermon. Something was going on in Easterbrook, something Thomas and Dora did not know about. They were still strangers here, and if there was open wrong-doing no one had told them. He turned over in his mind the seven deadly sins and a handful of the grosser civil crimes, and had to admit that he hadn't noticed anything out of the ordinary in Easterbrook. But the Rector thought there was and had told the village in no uncertain terms what he thought should be done about it. There was plenty of food for thought there.

Thomas turned over uneasily. There was also the strange matter of Sammy, the cat. How did he get in and out so mysteriously? Was the house not burglar proof after all? He really must go round the outside of it, looking at it from Sammy's point of view. He smiled gently to himself at the absurdity of the idea. He was still smiling gently when the scrunch of car tyres in the drive woke him two hours later.

A black car was standing before the front door, a black car so clean it could only belong to the police force. Thomas hurried downstairs. If there was one man he wanted to see it was Inspector Bream. He was standing on the bottom step of the staircase as Dora ushered him and Police-Constable Wilkins across the hall. From this slight eminence he was able to look down a little on the tall policeman.

"I'm sorry to have to disturb you like this on a Sunday afternoon, Mr. Harding, but it's a question of murder."

Thomas nodded. "Yes, I know. What's more—and this will surprise you, Inspector,—I know now who it was who was murdered. I found out on Friday."

"Really, sir?" said the Inspector drily. "I've known for some time who was murdered. It's the murderer I'm trying to catch."

"It won't be easy after all this time," said Thomas in doubtful tones.

"Oh, it's not hopeless," said the Inspector briskly. "He was seen here in Easterbrook yesterday and so he can't be far away. That's why I've come here. I would like permission to search your grounds and outbuildings for him."

Thomas stepped down to ground level with dignity.

"I am sorry, Inspector, I thought for a moment you were talking about the murdered skeleton I found here."

The Inspector gave a mirthless laugh. "I wish we were, sir. There's nothing I'd like so much as a real—begging your pardon, sir—cut and dried murder. No, I'm looking for one Alan Fenny in connection with the murder of his wife. You'll remember seeing it in the papers about the time you found your body."

"And why look here?" Dora spoke for the first time.

"He's an Easterbrook lad, Mrs. Harding, that's why. His mother still lives here and we thought he'd come back here if he was in trouble."

"And he did?"

"P.c. Wilkins here saw him in Easterbrook yesterday. He knows him by sight well enough on account of the lad having lived here for so long. We've been keeping an eye on his mother's cottage, of course, but he didn't make for that. He was over on the other side of the village when Wilkins saw him, and when he gave chase Fenny ran off towards the church." The Inspector paused dramatically.

"But he got away?"

"He got away, Mrs. Harding, because P.c. Wilkins began to have doubts about the church."

"Doubts about the church?" echoed Dora, to whom the phrase meant something quite different.

"He wondered whether he could apprehend anyone in a church. You know, the medieval idea that a person was safe in a church," said Bream sarcastically. "So he came to telephone me, and by the time he got back there with the Rector the church was empty."

P.c. Wilkins was so intent upon studying his boots that it was impossible to see his face.

"Would this have been some time about twelve o'clock?" asked Thomas suddenly.

"That's right," said Constable Wilkins.

"Why?" demanded Bream sharply.

"Because if it was, then I think I saw him too. I was in the church copying out some old benefactions—to do with the other murder—when a youngish man came in. He did look as if he'd been sleeping rough and he certainly hadn't shaved, but a pleasant enough manner."

"Yes, yes," urged the Inspector impatiently. "That would be him. He's been on the run for days now."

"Come to think of it, he did use the word sanctuary," said Thomas.

The Inspector snorted. "And what was he doing when you left, may I ask?"

"Praying. Do you want to look round the house, too, Inspector? You're very welcome. . . ."

"No, thank you, sir. That won't be necessary at this stage."

Thomas grinned. "Or in our priest's hole?"

"No thank you, sir."

Thomas did not offer to accompany the two policemen while they searched the grounds. They were not extensive, and beyond the old stable and the garden sheds, there was little room for anyone to hide. Instead he went to his usual chair in the drawing-room. P.c. Wilkins must have been extraordinary slow in going to ring the Inspector on Saturday. Hadn't Fenny mentioned waiting in the orchard for five minutes for the organist to leave the church?

The policemen declined tea when they had finished their search.

"We must get back to the green," said Inspector Bream. "We're using that as our rallying point."

"You're not alone then?"

"There's half the Calleford Constabulary going through this village with a toothcomb—and some of them aren't too keen on working Sunday afternoons either."

"There's just one thing puzzles me, Inspector."

Both men looked quickly at Thomas.

"If that man Fenny was in the church when I left and yet wasn't there when you arrived, he must have walked out of it in broad daylight, in the middle of the village. Didn't anyone see him? The village is busy enough at that time."

"Mr. Harding, I would not be surprised if a dozen people saw him." He looked sourly at Thomas. "What would surprise me is if any one of them would tell me. This village is nursing the extraordinary conviction that this man is innocent simply because they have known him since he was a boy. A murderer is someone you read about, not someone you know, so if you know someone he can't be a murderer."

"Do you think he's guilty?"

"I don't know. I don't need to know. I'm only a policeman and my job is to catch him. It's the judge's job to decide whether he's guilty—and the jury's, too, of course," he added, though without much conviction.

"You're bound to pick him up sooner or later," said Thomas. "It's too difficult to live in a small country like this without someone spotting you. He'll probably make for his mother's house one night."

"No, he won't," interjected Wilkins suddenly. "He may be a murderer but he's neither a fool nor one to get his mother into trouble. I'll bet my pension on that," he added hastily as the Inspector turned an enquiring gaze upon him.

"Ah," said Bream in a silky voice, "we mustn't forget that Constable Wilkins knows the accused. That should be a great help."

At ten o'clock on Monday morning Thomas was established in his chair in the drawing-room as usual. He had not been there long when Gladys came in to do her polishing. He watched her strong arms moving up and down for a minute or two and then asked her what she knew about the Barbary family.

"They're the people who used to have the Manor in olden times, aren't they? There's a lot of their tombs in the churchyard. We used to play amongst them when we was little." She fluffed out her duster. "There's the Barbary Charities, and those almshouses down by the river. There was the Barbary Bible that the head boy and girl at the school used to be given. They don't have those any longer, but my granny had one once. We've still got it at home."

"In the front parlour?"

"That's right, Mr. Harding. How did you know?"

"Go on about the Barbarys."

Gladys frowned. "I don't remember much more except that they gave a lot to the village. One of them built the school—you know before the government started. Not that the government have ever really got started on the school," she said frankly. "They just put up some huts each time we have a war and we have to make do with them."

"But the Barbarys gave them a building in the beginning to put the huts round?"

"That's right, Mr. Harding."

"Well, Gladys, you'll be interested to know that the body we found in that secret room was a Barbary. He was called Toby and the pathologist was right, he was fifteen when he was murdered."

"Oh, Mr. Harding, however did you find out?" Gladys stopped polishing and looked intently at the panelling. "To think of that poor boy lying there all those years and nobody knowing, and then you finding out all about him."

"Not all," said Thomas mildly. "I don't know who killed him yet."

"But you'll find out one day, won't you?" Gladys turned and faced him anxiously. "You're bound to discover who the real murderer was in the end, aren't you?"

"I hope so. The trail's a bit cold after a hundred and fifty years but I haven't given up trying yet."

"What are you going to do next, Mr. Harding?"

One of Gladys's great virtues as a worker was that she could work and listen at the same time. There is nothing so cramping to the conversational style of an employer as an employee who stops working when spoken to. Encouraged by her obvious attention and yet active muscles Thomas formulated his plans aloud.

"I had thought of getting in touch with the local history society—there must be one in an old place like Calleford. It occurred to me that they might like to come and see this secret room—and of course that they might have some records that might help me. Yes, I'll write to them this afternoon. I'd better have another good look in there myself. I really ought to do some research into the family history of the Barbarys as well, build up a background picture and so forth. I don't know anything like enough about the family or the house, and until I've got all the facts I can hardly expect to find a lead on the murderer."

"You mean who benefited from the murder and who lived here when it happened?" asked Gladys intelligently.

"That's right—and who was in a position to murder him. Of course, this was his own house which makes it easier in some ways—he would have been Sir Toby Barbary, you know, if he had lived another few weeks."

"Fancy!" exclaimed Gladys. "I must tell Mother that. She's ever so interested." She gave the woodwork a final sweep with her duster and gathered up her rags and polishes.

"That wood is coming up quite well, Gladys." Thomas inspected her polishing critically, something Dora would never have presumed to do. "Another few weeks and it'll be darker still."

"Every day helps, doesn't it?" she said brightly.

"By the way," said Thomas casually, as she made for the door, "can you tell me anything about Alan Fenny?"

She stiffened perceptibly. "The police say he murdered his wife."

"I know all that. I mean, what is he like as a person?"

"He's young," responded Gladys tonelessly. "He hadn't been married very long." She continued on her way to the door and was out of it before Thomas could ask her more. When she had gone Thomas dismissed Alan Fenny and

the present day from his mind and got out his notebook.
Ever since he had read that newspaper report on Friday,
events had conspired to keep him from thinking about the
Barbarys. Sermons, cats, police searches and a roving
murderer had had their share of attention over the week-
end. Now at last he was free to consider the skeleton.

He turned to a clean page in his book and made a neat
list of what he had so far discovered.

The body of a boy of fifteen who had been murdered
about a hundred and fifty years ago. (The pathologist's
evidence.)

A secret room which must have been a fixture of the
house soon after it was built. (The Rector thought it was a
genuine Jesuit priest's hole incorporated in the Tudor
Manor House by its original owners, but as the Barbarys
had owned the house at least since 1590 it was reasonable
to assume they knew all about the room.)

A family history which showed that a son called Toby
was born to Sir Toby Barbary, the 8th Baronet, and Fanny,
his wife, who died in his father's lifetime. (The Baronetage
in Calleford Library.)

That the son of this Sir Toby was christened Toby in
February 1800. (The Rector and the Parish Registers.)

That there was no record of this Toby being buried in
the parish. (The Rector and the Parish Registers; and the
choirboys and the churchyard.)

That this Toby disappeared one afternoon while fishing
in 1815, his fishing rod and shoe but not his body being
recovered from the river. (The Calleford *Courier.*) (Memo:
wrote Thomas, You can't believe everything you read in a
newspaper.)

That the boy disappeared while his father was away at
the wars, being killed at Waterloo a few weeks later. (The
Calleford *Courier.*)

That the boy's mother apparently left Easterbrook afterwards as her grave was not in the churchyard either.

That the 8th Baronet was succeeded by his brother, Sir
Richard, who was undoubtedly a great benefactor to the
parish. (The memorial tablets, Gladys, etc.) (Memo: from
Thomas to Thomas, What do you suppose that proves?)

Thomas paused in his writing. There was no doubt in

his own mind now that the skeleton was that of young Toby Barbary, that he had been murdered elsewhere and his body bundled into the secret room—no, that wasn't quite right. It hadn't been bundled. It had been placed there and the hands folded properly across the chest. That was what the pathologist had said. But his shoe—that had been thrown into the river with intent to mislead. The fishing rod had probably been carefully tied up in the trees at just the spot where it was most likely to be found. A nice piece of circumstantial evidence that—not conclusive but difficult to refute.

But why had the boy been murdered in the first place?

And why had the body been brought into the house when it could have gone into the river with much less trouble? After all, the boy's mother was presumably living here at the time and the father might have come back from the Continent at any moment.

If the 9th Baronet, Sir Richard, had murdered the boy in order to inherit the house and title, had he also planned the murder of his brother who was alive at the time? And when Napoleon had saved him the trouble, just lived happily ever after in Easterbrook devoting himself to the betterment of the villagers?

Somehow Thomas didn't think so.

Seven

THOMAS just could not settle to his afternoon rest that day. He tossed and turned uneasily on his bed, thinking resentfully of over-zealous doctors and over-anxious wives. He was not helped in his isolation by hearing sounds of voices downstairs. Dora would have fetched him for anything important, but it was maddening to lie in his room and not know who it was who was visiting the Manor.

Then the talking ceased and other, more confusing, sounds reached the bedroom. First odd bumps and scrapes and then, briefly, hammering.

Thomas bore this as long as he could and then put his legs to the ground, and, in a manner far from befitting the owner and master of the house, sidled along the upstairs landing. He could hear Dora chatting to someone in the study. He glanced at his wristwatch and decided to put on a bold front. Yawning ostentatiously he put his head round the study door.

"Tea ready yet, dear?" he asked. "Oh, good afternoon, Mr. Ford. I didn't know you were here."

"You said something about wanting that plug in the drawing-room shifted to beside the fireplace," said Charlie Ford, expertly twisting a length of cable, "so I nipped up today to get it started. I'm running it through from this power point in this room."

"I'd almost forgotten," admitted Thomas. "Finding that skeleton quite drove it from my mind."

"I've got the cable through into your cubby hole but there it will have to stay until I can get a matching switch for the other side." He stooped to give a final twist to a couple of screws. "By the way, I've left the ends of the wire bare in there so I don't think you'd better go in in case you get a shock. I've screwed up the entrance temporary like so you won't forget and go in by mistake."

Thomas nodded. "Tell me, what do you know about the Barbary family?"

Charlie scratched his head. "Not a lot, Mr. Harding. Wait a minute though—those almshouses were theirs, weren't they? Proper state they're in. As I tell the Rector, I do my best but they really do need money spending on them and the Rector tells me that there's just the same amount of money to keep them up now as there was a hundred and fifty years ago." He grinned expansively. "And a pound goes nowhere compared with before the war, does it, so you can guess how well they've been kept up, with labour being what it is."

"What else about the Barbarys?" prompted Thomas.

"I think they did something about the school but I don't remember exactly. I wasn't very fond of school," confessed Charlie. "I'll tell you something about them, though. One of 'em built the bridge over the river."

"Oh?" said Thomas, interested.

"When I was a lad we used to play in the water meadows down by the river, and if you come right up close near the bridge it's all written in a stone on the bridge about who built it and all that." The burly builder looked ruefully at his bulging tool kit and then at Thomas and said seriously, "Do you know, Mr. Harding, it must be thirty years since I had time to walk in them water meadows."

Thomas wanted to know why they had built a new bridge.

"Couldn't say, but I expect they had their reasons," said Charlie philosophically. "Anyway, it must have been a lot better than the old bridge. You can still see where it was, a good bit higher up the bank, of course, nearer the church. They altered the road, you know. I expect that had something to do with it."

Thomas nodded and said casually, "Now tell me something about this chap Alan Fenny."

Charlie Ford picked up his screwdriver. "Not a bad lad at all."

"Not a murderer?"

"Not a murderer," said Charlie quietly. "I've known him all his life. He was our opening batsman until he went to live in Calleford."

And murder wasn't cricket? thought Thomas. Aloud he said: "The police were here yesterday, looking for him."

The builder laughed. "Don't I know it. They poked their noses into everything in my yard. They even took a good look in a coffin I was making. I wish there had been someone in it—that would have given them a fright, right enough."

The next day was Tuesday. Thomas's plans for examining the secret room and writing to the local history society having been thwarted by Charlie Ford and his unfinished electrical wiring, he decided instead to visit the Rectory. He found the Rector in his study grappling with a buff coloured form of the shade favoured by Her Majesty's Commissioners of Inland Revenue.

He waved it in front of Thomas. "Matthew has never been one of my favourite saints, Mr. Harding."

"You're willing to render unto Caesar all right but he makes it difficult?" suggested Thomas.

"Exactly. You would think a dilapidations claim would be straightforward, wouldn't you?" said the Rector plaintively, pointing to a crumbling coping stone clearly visible from the study window. Thomas followed his gaze to a neo-Gothic stone corbel which leered back at them.

"Rather the worse for wear," agreed Thomas.

"I believe 'weathered' is the correct expression," murmured Mr. Martindale, "but these people don't seem to understand."

"Perhaps I could help?"

"Would you? I'd be delighted. I've got as far as Part 5 where it says don't answer if you've completed Part 2 (A) but I want to say something in both places."

Thomas took the form and was glad he didn't work for the Inland Revenue. It was the better part of an hour before he had sorted out the Rectory claim and was able to push it across to the Rector for his signature.

"Splendid," pronounced the clergyman happily. "I

usually have to write them several times before we get it straight. Now what did you come to see me about?"

"The skeleton. It *was* the same Toby you found in the Parish Registers who was christened in 1800. He disappeared in 1815 while he was fishing and his body was never found. I discovered a report in the Calleford *Courier*, just before the news that his father was killed at Waterloo."

The Rector nodded solemnly. "Why was he supposed to have been fishing?"

"Someone saw him on the river bank that afternoon and someone else found his fishing rod tangled in some trees and his shoe in the water. And I found him with his skull bashed in in my drawing-room."

"He could have been fishing."

"But why didn't whoever killed him push his body into the river? Why did they go to all those lengths to conceal him in the house and then plaster over the walls?"

"I think I know the reason for that. There used to be an old mill about a quarter of a mile downstream. The mill dam is still there though they don't use it any more. A body would be more or less certain to fetch up there, and if it had had its skull—er—bashed in then that would be bound to be noticed, even in those days."

Thomas was silent for a moment, then he said, "Then the fact that the body wasn't found in the mill dam would be suspicious, too."

"Yes."

"But *The Courier* didn't even mention the mill dam."

"*The Courier* would only be read by a very few people in Easterbrook. The parson, the schoolmaster—if they had one—and the Barbary family themselves. The paper wouldn't hint at a scandal without proof, especially in a local family as highly thought of as the Barbary's."

"So the local people might have wondered after all."

"Most certainly. But even if they had wondered I don't think they would have done anything more. The squire's family were a great deal more important then than they are now." He smiled ruefully. "So was the parson. It would have been as much as your job was worth to have wondered out loud."

"If that's so," said Thomas, "it answers one point and half another."

"The other half being?"

"Charlie Ford's grandfather."

"Charlie Ford's grandfather?"

"He knew about the secret room. He could have known about the body. If people could have been suspicious at the time those suspicions could have been passed down. Obadiah Ford would have been a boy in the 1870s. *His* grandfather could well have wondered why that body wasn't found in the mill dam."

Mr. Martindale stared out of the window. "So you know who your body was, when he was murdered and that someone tried to make it seem like accidental death, but you don't know the most important thing yet."

"I don't know who killed him."

"You don't know why he was killed. That is what you need to know, Mr. Harding. When you find out why he was killed you will know who killed him. And his murder, though still a tragedy, will at least make sense. If you only discover the murderer the picture will be incomplete for ever." He withdrew his gaze from the window and looked seriously at Thomas. "It is the same here in Easterbrook now. It is not only a question of discovering the murderer but of finding the motive. Only then can we come to terms with tragedy."

"It's difficult to think of a reason for killing a fifteen-year-old boy," responded Thomas. "His father was still alive and healthy at the time and no one can have been sure he would be killed. There seems to have been plenty of money in the family too—judging from the amount Sir Richard gave away."

"Find the motive and you'll find the murderer," insisted the Rector.

Thomas protested, "That's more easily said than done. I don't even know where to begin."

"With his family."

Thomas looked up sharply. In anyone else he would have suspected cynicism but the Rector's face was lined and sad.

"His father was away at the time so it can't have been

him. I can't trace his mother at all. She doesn't seem to be in the churchyard. An uncle inherited, Sir Richard, and he seems to have devoted himself to good works. He's the only one I can find out much about. He might have been a wicked uncle, I suppose," said Thomas doubtfully.

The Rector coughed drily. "There is a precedent."

"It's just that the good he has done has lived on in memorials and plaques and not died with him," said Thomas, pleased at his own aptness.

The rector did not smile. "It is not given us to know, Mr. Harding. The evil may have lived on too." He looked round his book-lined walls and then said kindly, "I think you'll have to leave stone memorials and try written historical records now."

"I'm not a scholar. . . ."

"You're a searcher after truth, Mr. Harding," pronounced the Rector warmly, "and that's much more important." ˌ

The next two days dragged uncomfortably slowly for Thomas. Charlie Ford had indeed screwed up the entrance to the priest's hole, and Thomas found it irritating to sit in the drawing-room and not be able to get in there. Alan Fenny was still at large, and though Sammy, the cat, made no more spectacular reappearances in the wrong places, the atmosphere in the village was still tense.

Thomas was therefore quite relieved to be setting out with Dora on the Friday for their weekly shopping expedition to Calleford. He left Dora in the grocer's debating the merits of two rival cheeses and made his way to the public library, giving the Rose and Crown an affectionate wave as he went between them and up the library steps.

He made for the section labelled "Calleford and Calleshire", meaning to begin his researches with the better-known histories of the county but was at once led astray by a book whose title caught his eye.

It was a history of the County Regiment. Thomas took it down from the shelf and turned the pages back. It had been written in the 1890s by the then colonel. Thomas quickly scanned the contents and felt a momentary pang of sympathy for the author. It must have been very difficult to have been colonel of a regiment which had not drawn a sword in anger for forty years.

Thomas settled himself in a chair and began to read about the 123rd or Calleshire Regiment. Their beginnings were obscure but they fought well at Blenheim, covered themselves with glory at Waterloo and emerged with as much credit as anyone else from the Crimean War. And in 1872 they were amalgamated with another regiment of the line. It was quite clear from his foreword that the author regarded this as a fate worse than court-martial, and would have preferred to have seen every man-jack of them slain by tribesmen from the North-West Frontier.

Waterloo had been the regiment's finest hour and its colonel, Sir Toby Barbary, had shared in it to the full. They had fought against Marshal Ney in the desperate battle of Quatre-Bras on the Brussels-Charleroi road on Friday, June 16th, 1815, and were obliged to retire with heavy losses to Waterloo. They were attacked there with the rest of the British Army by Napoleon's forces two days later.

They fought all day that long Sunday, and always where the fight was at its thickest. At seven o'clock in the evening Napoleon ordered forward the Imperial Guard and after them launched his last cavalry reserve. Then Wellington commanded the whole British line to advance. The Calleshire Regiment, led by their colonel, went forward to a man. Sir Toby fell in the advance against the Imperial Guard, still at the head of his men.

"He died happy in the knowledge that the regiment had done its duty and that right would prevail," wrote his Victorian chronicler, eighty years after the dust of battle had died away.

Thomas doubted it.

Resolution was the only sentiment he knew bred on the bloody field of war. Certainly not happiness. And Sir Toby Barbary cannot have gone happily to his death so soon after the mysterious death of his only son. Did this writer know about that?

He leafed through the book until he happened upon a brief biography of Sir Toby. The parts played by the man in his time were conscientiously listed by the author:

soldier, landowner, baronet, Justice of the Peace, scholar . . .

Thomas hadn't expected that one and looked more closely.

"Colonel Sir Toby Barbary was in his own way a man of letters, and in 1812 had had privately printed a short history of his own family which had been founded in Elizabethan times."

There was no mention of his son.

Thomas beamed. A family history written by one of the Barbarys was an unexpected find. It would be a great help in filling in the background picture though not, alas, likely to give a lead on the murderer. 1812 was too early to hope for that. At the very least though it would save him hours of research. The next thing to do was to find it.

This time fate was on Thomas's side.

"We're sure to have it," said the junior assistant whom he approached. "After all, Easterbrook is very near here and we're more likely to have a copy than anyone else." She bent over some card index cabinets and emerged with a white card. She led the way confidently to a shelf and presented him with a slim volume bound in calf.

Thomas turned back the flyleaf eagerly. That excellent institution, the Calleford Public Library, had had this copy bequeathed to them by a noted and reverend antiquarian of Victorian days, and in the true library tradition had given it shelf space ever since.

It had been privately printed for Sir Toby Barbary of Easterbrook by one Peter Billings, a Printer, at his Press in Ox Lane, Calleford in 1812.

Thomas turned instinctively to the end but was disappointed. Sir Toby had finished his family history with the death of his father, the 7th Baronet, in 1779, and the birth of his son in January 1800. With a reticence seemly in a nineteenth-century English gentleman, he had made little mention of himself in his record of his family. Instead he had craved the indulgence of readers for burdening them with yet another book, and he ventured to hope that the story of an ordinary English family might interest them.

Thomas turned back to the beginning and began to read the story of the Barbarys.

The first of his forbears whom Sir Toby had been able to trace was a certain small merchant on Cheapside. He was the grandfather of the first baronet and a man of business who had prospered. He had passed on his profits and his business ability to his son who had prospered exceedingly. *His* son, later the first Sir Toby, had had both the money and the courage to take risks with valuable cargoes on the high seas. He had been successful in his daring ventures, and soon had enough money to pass over that peculiarly English barrier which separates trade from landed property.

And in 1587 he had done what all men who make money do. He had bought himself a fine house in the country. Well primed by his profits on the high seas, money continued to pour into the purse of Mr. Barbary and in 1590, when one of his ships was able to perform some slight service to Her Majesty, Queen Elizabeth, his cup was full. He was rewarded with a baronetcy.

"An honour which came as a great surprise and delight to him," ran the text. Thomas could not forbear to smile at that.

Here the family record broke off to tell the story of the house which the Barbary family had bought, and Thomas read it closely.

It had belonged until 1587 to a Roman Catholic family called Cloake, who in that year had had all their goods and two thirds of their lands seized because of their failure to pay fines imposed on them for recusancy.

Thomas reached for his notebook, not displeased. The secret room had been too well made to be anything but a genuine priest's hole. He read on carefully. Where Elizabethan policies had been kind to the Barbarys of England they had been harsh indeed to the Cloakes and other Catholics.

They had suffered first, though lightly compared with what was to come, under the Act of Uniformity in 1559. By 1581 they were paying fines of £20 a month for recusancy and paying another 100 marks for attending Mass, with an ever-present risk of imprisonment too. By 1587 they were ruined and Mr. Barbary of Cheapside, whose fortunes had risen as theirs had fallen, was able to buy their family home.

"For a song," decided Thomas in parenthesis. "Barbary had his head screwed on and the Cloakes weren't in a position to bargain with anybody."

The family historian (a Barbary) had skated delicately round this point, devoting himself to a description of the house.

"The Manor was a well-known Catholic one of those times, ideal for the purpose of secret worship on account of its secluded position in a small village. It was near enough, too, to the coast, where Jesuits who had come privily by night from France might come before daylight came to show them as strangers. I have been unable to learn who built the house, but the handiwork of Nicholas. . . ."

But the words on the following page did not complete this interesting sentence. Thomas looked closely at the old book and then sat back in his chair.

Two pages of text had been most skilfully removed from the family history of the Barbarys.

Eight

"No, not torn out. Cut out very carefully, I should say," said Thomas, prodding his fork into a piece of plaice without enthusiasm. Both the chicken and the lamb had been off the menu by the time he arrived at The Tabard, and he was not fond of fish.

"So there must have been a clue in them," said Dora eagerly.

"No," said her husband placidly.

"No? But. . . ."

"Not a clue to the murder, my dear. This book was written in 1812 and the murder wasn't committed until 1815."

Dora looked so downcast that Thomas relented. "What they *will* have had in them was a piece about that secret room."

"That helps, doesn't it?" she said slowly. "I mean it proves that whoever knew about the room knew about the book as well."

"And whoever did the murder removed those pages, would you say?"

Dora looked distressed. "So the murderer was an educated man, someone who could read and who would think about the book too."

"I hadn't thought of it like that."

There was a pause and then Dora said, "It's funny, you know, I'd always hoped in my own mind that Toby had been murdered by some ruffian or other for money. This makes it seem much worse—a calculated murder."

"I may be wrong about those missing pages, but a description of our priest's hole is the most likely thing to be on them and the most likely reason for removing them, too. What we must do is to go back and see if it is mentioned in any other book in the library. If it isn't then you can bet your life the murderer cut those two pages out because they told the world all about it." He pushed his plate away. "Let's not wait for coffee. We've plenty of time if we hurry."

"Thomas Harding, you are hurrying nowhere." She regarded him with mock severity. "Have you forgotten you are an invalid?"

He grinned sheepishly. "I had, rather. There just doesn't seem time to feel ill at the moment."

They went back to the Calleford Library together. The Local History shelves were pleasantly full.

The first book they came to was entitled: *A Perambulation of the County conteining the Description, Hystorie, and Customes of the Shire Written in the Yeere 1569*.

There was no mention of Easterbrook in it.

"The murderer didn't have anything to fear from that one," commented Thomas, taking down the next book.

This was *A Topographie or Survey of the County with some Chronological, Historical, and other Matters touching the same: and several Parishes and Places therein*, dated 1689, and containing several pages of dedication to the Nobility, Gentry and Commonalty of the County.

Easterbrook was described in this as lying four miles towards the north-east distant from Calleford, in the Bailiwick of Lampard, in the Lathe of St. Thomas and in the Deanery and Diocese of Calleford.

There was no mention of the Manor in it.

"History is not very clear, is it?" said Dora, poring over the long old-fashioned s's.

"They weren't too good at measuring," admitted Thomas, taking down the next book. "Listen to this one. 'The Parish of Easterbrook is situated for the most part very low and unpleasant about two miles north of Calleford.'"

"Two miles," echoed Dora. "That other book said four."

"Ah, but this one was written over a hundred years later—in 1780 to be precise."

"And how many miles is Easterbrook from Calleford then?"

"Then and now and to be precise—three."

"Idiot," said Dora affectionately. "What book is that anyway?"

"One of the standard histories of the county. Not very kind to Easterbrook, is it? 'Very low and unpleasant', indeed! I say, listen to this. There's a bit about the Manor House. 'There is a Manor House which is the residence of the Barbarys of Easterbrook. It has been lately much deformed by some modern windows put in different parts of it.'"

"The big bedroom and the dining-room," cried Dora. "I knew it. Those windows are quite different from the others. They're not modern enough."

"They were in 1780. That's not all. Listen. 'It was formerly the home of the Cloake family who were imprisoned for Popish practices in 1587. Below the village is an ancient fulling-mill and adjoining to it a newly erected cornmill.'"

"What," asked Dora inevitably, "is a fulling mill?"

"A process of cleansing cloth. Beating and washing it." He read on from the book. "'A fair is held yearly on Mayday. A court leet and court baron is held for this manor.' And there's a detailed history of the Church from 1295," he went on hurriedly; he did not know what courts leet or baron were.

The last books on the shelf were a comprehensive study of the County in twelve stoutly bound volumes. Easterbrook was in volume three. This author had no strong views on the distance of Easterbrook from Calleford. What had impressed him most about the village in 1821 was its new bridge.

"'A new bridge of brickwork, which consists of three arches, has been lately built here on the Calle by voluntary subscription headed by Sir Richard Barbary, Bart., divers gentlemen of the county and other persons, who resort to Crowden and other places beyond.

"'The Church is an ancient large structure, that has nothing peculiarly remarkable in it. The bishop is patron of this rectory valued in the king's books at 131l. 1s. 8d.

"'The manor house is old, and a large, irregular brick and timber structure. It was formerly the home of the

Catholic family of Cloake who were taken by the pursuivants in 1587. Since then the Barbarys have lived there.'"

"Not a thing about a secret room," said Dora, when
Thomas had done. "He was lucky, wasn't he? I mean he
could hardly go around tearing pages out of all the books
in the library."

"They wouldn't have been in the library then," said
Thomas absently. "He must have cut it out of them when
they were somewhere else. And the earlier writers may
not have known about it at all. It's quite likely that that
room was forgotten about for a couple of hundred years,
and only found again when Sir Toby the 8th came to do
some research for his history."

"Then those first three writers wouldn't have known to
put it in their books, but what about this last one?"

"By 1821," said Thomas grimly, "steps had been taken
so that no one knew about it. The wall had been plastered
over and mention of it removed from the family history."

"But what about people talking? The murderer can't
have been the only person to have known—especially if it
had been written about in that family history."

Thomas snapped the last of the county histories shut.
"They must have talked. Obadiah Ford wouldn't have
known about the room if they hadn't. But they would only
talk amongst themselves, you know. There were no police
to talk to in 1815."

It seemed to Thomas that nowadays Saturday morning
always found him in the village. Certainly since the skeleton had been discovered he had forsaken his chair in the
drawing-room on Saturdays and been none the worse for
it. This Saturday was no exception, for he decided that it
was about time, he had a close look at the Barbary
Almshouses.

He had seen them in the distance often enough, but
until now they had just been six very small cottages
huddled together by the river. He walked down past The
George, the village's only pub, and the church towards the
river Calle. The cottages were so near the river they were
nearly in it. Thomas decided that the early historian who
described Easterbrook "for the most part very low and

unpleasant" wasn't so far wide of the mark after all. The
cottages were pleasant enough to look at now—many a
town dweller would say they were picturesque—but in
winter they must be damp and cold.

There were six of them, all joined together in one row,
each with its own front door and single bedroom. They
were of deep, mellowed, red brick, with a heavy gable at
each end. Exactly in the middle was a stone set in the
brick on which was engraved the year, 1816, and a rather
worn monogram. Thomas consulted his notebook. This
must have been the first of the many benefactions of Sir
Richard. He was about to advance a little nearer the
almshouses, the better to see the monogram, when the
door of the right-hand end cottage opened and a woman
emerged carrying a cup of tea.

Thomas stood still. He had been very careful not to
seem to be staring and he did not know the woman. She
walked through the tiny garden of the cottage towards
Thomas and a thick hedge which edged the road from the
village. She was almost abreast of Thomas when she
addressed the hedge.

"A cup of tea for you, Jack Wilkins."

Thomas turned to see a greatly discomfited policeman
poke his head through the leaves.

"Go on, take it," she urged. "Mr. Harding here won't
tell the Inspector, will you, Mr. Harding?"

"Er—no—madam, certainly not," said Thomas. "If
you'd be so kind as to tell me what I'm not to tell him,
that is."

"That Constable Wilkins accepted refreshment from
Alan Fenny's mother when he was watching her house."
She had a curiously harsh voice for a woman, and odd,
disconnected clothes. "There's no question of dereliction
of duty, he's still keeping it under observation, aren't you,
Jack Wilkins?"

"Now, now, Mrs. Fenny, it's just that I know as well as
you do that Alan will not come here. The Inspector can't
be expected to understand that. He hasn't ever met Alan."

"Maybe." The woman appeared a little mollified by this
and turned to Thomas. "But you have met him, Mr.
Harding, haven't you? How was he?"

"I only saw him for a moment or two in the church," said Thomas cautiously. "He was tired and he hadn't shaved for a day or so, but he wasn't looking ill or anything."

"He's not doing himself any good, hiding up like this," ventured the police constable.

"The police aren't doing him much good not looking for the murderer," she responded tartly. "Wasting their time watching this house instead of tracking down whoever strangled his wife."

"Perhaps if he gave himself up they would do just that," said Thomas unwillingly. Mrs. Fenny could not have been further from anybody's mental image of a poor widow, living on charity in an almshouse, whose only son had got himself in trouble with the police. She stood there in the sunlight, her grey hair scraped back into a severe bun, glaring at them both through steel-rimmed spectacles.

She treated Thomas's feeble suggestion with contempt. "It's my belief Alan knows who did it and he wants to settle the score himself."

"That's why the Rector wants him in gaol then," burst out Thomas, with sudden understanding.

"Aye," she said. "To save him from really committing murder."

"And don't you?"

"I would rather he was punished for that than for a murder he didn't do."

Thomas began to see why it was that the village of Easterbrook was convinced of Alan Fenny's innocence.

"Now you know that's not true, Mrs. Fenny," interposed P.c. Wilkins. "What you want is Alan safe and sound and free to walk about the village again."

"I want the real murderer caught and I don't care who catches him." She turned a bleak eye on Thomas. "They tell me you are a great one for solving murder mysteries, Mr. Harding. Perhaps you could find out who killed my son's wife."

"Mine's an old murder," he said hastily. "It happened over a hundred and fifty years ago. I only poke about in old books and so forth; nothing serious, you know."

"I should have said murder was always serious." She

took back the policeman's empty cup. "Wouldn't you, Mr. Wilkins?"

"Always," agreed Wilkins, gravely. "Thank you for the tea, Mrs. Fenny. It's thirsty work doing nothing."

She brushed his thanks aside ungraciously.

"At least you know Alan well enough to agree he's not likely to come here. Ah, here comes Mr. Cousens."

Both men turned to see the organist stepping over the green from the church.

"He looks in every day to know if there is any news. He knew them both so well when they were in the choir."

Mrs. Fenny left them and went to greet him. Cousens nodded in their direction, and then went inside the cottage with Mrs. Fenny. Thomas inclined his head towards the almshouses.

"A very unusual woman that."

"You're telling me. Her only son on the run for murder and in this village somewhere for sure and he hasn't been near her house. We've had it watched ever since they found the body. And she also knows he won't come here."

"And she knows he didn't do it."

"Or she's a good actress," agreed the constable. "Told the Inspector straight that she'd brought her son up properly and that did not include strangling his wife, and that, as far as she was concerned, was the end of it. Then she showed him the door, literally, and he went. A mistake that," he said reflectively. "The Inspector didn't take kindly to her."

"She's a strong character all right."

"Mr. Harding, who did you tell that you had seen Alan Fenny in the church last Saturday?"

Thomas looked up. "Nobody."

"That's what I thought," said the constable.

"I didn't even know it was Alan Fenny," said Thomas, "until I spoke to you and the Inspector on Sunday afternoon. And then, if you remember, the Inspector asked me to keep quiet about it."

"I remember all right," said Wilkins.

"I didn't mention it to anyone at all. I don't think it occurred to me to—there's only my wife and she knew anyway."

"No." Wilkins nodded towards the almshouses. "You realise she knew you'd seen him, don't you?"

"How do you know?"

"She asked you how he was looking—remember?"

"So she did," said Thomas looking appreciatively at the young constable. "So she's either seen him herself or . . ."

"Or spoken to someone else who has seen him since Saturday."

Thomas found his contact with Mrs. Fenny curiously disturbing. He could not get her gaunt figure and grating voice out of his mind all that day and the next. The Barbary murder, which had happily absorbed all his attention until now, suddenly seemed dry-as-dust when compared with the strangling of a young wife, the flight of her fugitive husband and the attitude of his proud, intimidating mother. Yet he found the police point of view eminently reasonable. When a beautiful young woman is found strangled in bed after a quarrel with her husband and when that husband chooses to avoid the police, the police cannot be blamed for suspecting him.

He said all this to Dora several times that Sunday. She listened like the dutiful wife she was and offered no argument save that of reminding him that the village of Easterbrook considered him innocent.

"So innocent that they are prepared to shelter him here somewhere," she pointed out.

"That's another thing I'm uneasy about. I'm beginning to be afraid that Alan Fenny is not hiding here in Easterbrook just to escape the police. He could have done that more easily in London than here, where everyone knows him."

"You mean he's come back to Easterbrook for a reason?"

"It's a possibility one cannot overlook." Thomas tended to become pedantic when worried.

"So if he didn't do the murder himself you think he means to catch the person who did?"

"Yes."

Dora's reaction was spirited. "I don't blame him. The police aren't trying to find anyone else. Why shouldn't he?"

He remained gloomy. "I only hope his mother doesn't know who did it even if he does. She would be in great danger if she did."

Altogether it was quite a relief to them both when Monday morning arrived and with it the deeds of Easterbrook Manor.

The firm of Puckle, Puckle and Nunnery, Solicitors, had been most reluctant to part with these—even to their own client. They didn't like letting them out of their sight, let alone out of the City of London. It had taken several persuasive letters from Thomas to get them to entrust anything as valuable as the deeds of a house to Her Majesty's Mails, and they had nearly refused pointblank when they learnt that Thomas wished to see them out of curiosity. The senior partner (the first Mr. Puckle reading from left to right) had been most pained at this and devoted two whole paragraphs to assuring Thomas that the deeds had been scrutinized with the utmost care before the completion of the purchase took place. Of all the flimsy pretexts they had ever heard, that of a client wishing to consult the deeds himself was apparently the flimsiest, and Mr. Puckle devoted two more paragraphs to saying so.

"Did they think Gladys was going to light the fire with them?" growled Thomas, "or Dora make a lampshade of the parchment?"

Thomas broke the seals on the bulky parcel and promptly forgot about Puckle, Puckle and Nunnery.

He was on his hands and knees on the drawing-room floor and surrounded by paper when Dora found him three hours later.

"Be careful where you tread," he warned her unnecessarily. "There are deeds everywhere."

"So I see."

"I had to put them somewhere and the floor was the only place that was big enough."

"What's this one?" Dora pointed to a document brown with age, that was lying nearest to the door.

Thomas picked it up and unfolded it with great care. It crackled audibly as he did so.

"I think, only think, mind you, that this is the oldest thing here."

"When the Barbarys bought it from the Cloakes?"

"That's right. When Gerald Cloake, Gentleman, sold out to Tobias Barbary, City gent."

Dora peered at the old paper. "I can't read it."

"Neither can I. I'm only guessing because it's the oldest in sight."

His wife held the writing close to her eyes. "The ink's quite brown and what tiny writing. Very neat though."

"Italic," said Thomas, "but I can't even tell whether it's in English or Latin. Now these later ones are a bit easier to read. I've put them in chronological order round the room, starting with this old one."

"What comes next?"

"Nothing much until they sold some land off in 1650."

"Where?"

"As far as I can make out it was a bit the other side of the river, but they bought it back again about a hundred years later."

"A ship coming home?"

"They probably found they needed more of the river water," said Thomas wisely. "I can just about make out the writing, but making sense of it is another matter. Listen to this: 'That desmesne, messuage and hereditament situate on the north east side of the river Calle from the bridge to the mill being twenty-four acres and seven rods'."

"And when did they sell the lot?"

Thomas pointed to an impressive pile of paper in front of the fireplace.

"1871. It's all here. The estate was entailed by the first Sir Toby when he was made a baronet to heirs male of the body male. And it lasted that way until Sir Walter, the 10th Baronet, died in 1870, without any children."

"Sir Richard's son."

"That's right. When Walter died the estate and the title passed to his cousin Theodore in America—the one I found in that Baronetage those fierce old ladies . . ."

"The Misses Siskin," supplied Dora.

"The Misses Siskin lent you. Do you remember?"

She nodded. "Bertam's son," she quoted from memory.

"We wondered why he didn't come back when he inherited."

Thomas picked up his notebook. "That's right. Bertram must have been the younger brother of both the last Sir Toby and Sir Richard. He went to America and his son inherited from Sir Richard's son."

"And didn't come back when he did so," said Dora again.

"Not only did he not come back," said Thomas, "but he sold the property just as soon as he could. In 1871 to be exact, and as his cousin Walter only died in 1870 and he was three thousand miles away he couldn't have been much quicker about it."

"I thought you couldn't break an entail?"

"You can with the consent of your son, if he's over twenty-one. Theodore had a son called Eugene whose name we found in that little Baronetage too. There's a formidable document in that pile there breaking the entail."

"What happened then?"

"The estate was broken up. The farms were sold to the tenants mostly and the house was just left with enough land for one farm." Thomas pointed to a copy of an old conveyance. "That was sold off a bit later. Now there's just the house and garden."

"That's a blessing anyway." She looked across the floor. "And are those all changes of ownership since the Barbarys?"

"They are. Your friends were right. There are twelve of them. The last one of all records the purchase of the Manor by one Thomas Harding, City gent. The paper looks very white, doesn't it?"

"I'm sure Puckle, Puckle and Nunnery only use the best," murmured Dora. She surveyed her drawing-room floor. "Is Bertram suspect too?"

Thomas sat back on his heels.

"Well, I should like to know when he went to America and why."

"And why his son didn't come back either. I should have thought it would have been the natural thing."

"Yes indeed. By the way, do you know where Yew Tree Cottage, Easterbrook, is?"

Dora frowned. "In between here and The George, I

think. I believe a Miss Casterton—yes that's the name—
she lives there. Isn't it that little timber cottage that's
rather tucked away? Why?"

"The benevolent Sir Richard gave it away."

"*Gave* it away?"

"That's right. I found a Deed of Gift tucked in one of
these bundles."

"He was an exceptionally generous man," she said
lightly, tucking her arm affectionately in his. "You have a
lot to live up to here, but in the meantime what about
some lunch?"

Thomas climbed stiffly to his feet.

"Who did he give it to?" asked Dora casually.

Thomas rummaged about among the paper on the floor.

"I didn't look. Ah, here it is."

He handed her a stiff wad of paper covered in faded
copperplate writing.

"A Deed of Gift," read Dora aloud, "conveying the—the
des . . . the what?"

"Desmesne," suggested Thomas.

"Desmesne, messuage and hereditament of the freehold
land and building known as Yew Tree Cottage,
Easterbrook, to—oh, it was only to a tenant. Isn't copperplate nice to look at?"

"Who was the tenant?" asked Thomas on his way to the
door. "Does it mention his name?"

Dora peered down the page, "Somewhere it does—I
saw it. Here it is. Shambrook, Giles Shambrook."

"Who?" shouted Thomas.

"Giles Shambrook. What are you shouting about? It's a
funny name, I know but . . ."

He clutched her arm in excitement. "Don't you realise
who Giles Shambrook was?"

"A tenant," said Dora sensibly. "It says so here."

"He was also," said Thomas, suddenly sober, "the last
man to see our Toby Barbary alive."

"No!"

"That was the name of the man who said he saw Toby
Barbary fishing by the river that afternoon."

Nine

Tuesday was a cold, bright day. Thomas established himself in his study by the fire. He had one letter to answer and two more to write.

The one to be answered had arrived that morning from a Mr. Archibald Mellon, who described himself in a flowing script as the Honorary Secretary of the Calleshire County Archaeological and Historical Society. It has come to the notice of the Society through a report in the columns of the Calleford *Courier* that Mr. Harding was the owner of a secret room and an ancient skeleton. Would he, wrote Mr. Mellon, be prepared to countenance a visit from a member of the society with a view to investigating these interesting discoveries? The object of the Society was to further all manner of inquiry into and preservation of objects and records to do with the history of the County of Calleshire, and he was sure they could count upon the cooperation of Mr. Harding in their work.

They could.

"I have, I believe," wrote Thomas modestly, "discovered a genuine priest's hole in a house which belonged to a Catholic family in Elizabethan times. I myself know nothing about the subject but would be very happy to show the secret hiding place to any of your members who would be interested."

That at least he felt he owed to the experts in historical research.

The second letter was to the admirable Miss Porteous who had been his private secretary in London. He wanted to buy a copy of the Barbary family history for himself.

Thomas was not a second-hand book buyer himself and had no very clear idea of how the second-hand book trade worked, but he was confident that Miss Porteous would know. Miss Porteous always knew. Because Miss Porteous always knew Thomas's successors had persuaded her to overcome her natural inclinations to leave the firm when Thomas did. It had cost them an astonishing amount of money.

Thomas felt quite nostalgic as he wrote out the old familiar address.

The third letter took up the rest of the morning and was written on thin airmail paper to an address in Detroit, U.S.A.

Thomas chose his words with care. It wasn't easy to write to a man you had never seen and tell him you had found the family skeleton in the family cupboard, but it had to be done because Thomas needed to know just when Bertram Barbary had emigrated to the United States. Had he gone well and truly before the murder? Had he gone precipitately immediately afterwards? Or had he just emigrated years later to seek his fortune in the land of promise?

There was another point too. Had he and his descendants done so well in that young country that the landed property of Easterbrook with its long family associations meant nothing to them? Or were those associations centred round the body of a young boy of fifteen, murdered with a cruel blow and stuffed through a hole in the panelling?

"Of course, this Sir Thaddeus may know nothing at all," he said to Dora at luncheon. "Perhaps they don't go in for family histories and that sort of thing much over there."

"Oh, don't they!" said Dora crisply. "That's where you're wrong, Thomas Harding. They go in for them like anything. Besides, even if they didn't..."

"Yes?"

"This man, Sir Thaddeus, he's still English, isn't he? I mean it's only the women in the family who were American, isn't it?"

Thomas let this go and returned to the matter of Yew Tree Cottage.

"I would like to know if Bertram had a hand in the giving of that cottage of Giles Shambrook before he went

to America. That Deed of Gift might just as well have had
'for services rendered' written across the top."

"Does that mean that Shambrook was the murderer?"

"I can't say. A small cottage is not much of a reward for
murder but it might well be the price of silence. I'm
prepared to bet it wasn't one of the most publicised of the
good Sir Richard's benefactions. I'm going down to have a
look at it this afternoon."

"After your rest," stated Dora.

"After my rest," agreed Thomas amiably.

It was about half past four therefore when Thomas set
out for the centre of the village. He was just nearing the
church when he spotted Charlie Ford walking across the
village green. He was the one man Thomas wanted to see.
He had been trying to get hold of him for several days now
to get him to come and finish his wiring job. Thomas
wanted to get inside the priest's hole again himself and
now the County History Society were coming too.

Unconsciously Thomas quickened his pace after Charlie
Ford, but barely half a minute later he was struggling to
get his breath. He stopped then, fulminating against his
weak heart. By the time he had got his breath back,
Charlie Ford was out of sight. He walked on, more slowly,
hoping to catch him somewhere between the church and
The George.

He walked along the churchyard wall, keeping his eyes
well open, but could see no sign of the builder. He turned
the corner by the public house. There was nobody
resembling Charlie Ford whom he could see. Thomas
retraced his steps for a little and peered about him.
Charlie Ford seemed to have disappeared completely. He
would have to telephone the man instead.

He turned towards the post office with his letters.

"Good day to you, Mr. Harding," said a harsh voice
behind him.

"Mrs. Fenny! I didn't expect to see you."

Her strong features mocked him. "Why not? I was only
under observation—not arrest."

Thomas was every bit as confused as she had meant him
to be, and murmured an apology.

She bowed. "Tell me, are you any nearer to finding your murderer?"

"I think I am," admitted Thomas cautiously. "I was lucky enough to find some fresh evidence yesterday which is throwing a little new light on the crime."

"I'm glad to hear it." She paused and glanced quickly over her shoulder. "I think I can say the same about our murderer, too. Alan won't have to hide for ever, you know." She flashed him a triumphant smile and made for the door of the post office.

"Mrs. Fenny," said Thomas urgently, "if you know something you should go to the police. You are in grave danger if you don't."

She looked down her nose and said in her peculiar grating voice, "I'm not afraid, Mr. Harding. It's the murderer who should be afraid."

"Your son mustn't take the law into his own hands. If you know something you should go to the police now. Besides, Alan may be in danger too."

Mrs. Fenny looked at him, a crooked smile playing on her thin lips. "I don't think we need worry about Alan, Mr. Harding. He's safe enough. And he'll go to the police all right when he's got all the evidence he needs to prove someone else killed Mary."

Thomas opened his mouth to speak—but Mrs. Fenny, with her own curious aplomb, had walked away. Thomas was more disturbed than he would have cared to admit by his encounter, and he went on his way with his mind on the fugitive Alan Fenny and his odd mother.

He found Yew Tree Cottage where Dora had described it, up a narrow lane behind The George and the church. It was an old cottage. Thomas would have put it at least as old as the Manor, but not so well maintained. It was brick and timber, too, and one of the outer walls bulged uncomfortably. It was far from tumbledown though, and its garden obviously well cared for. There were several yew trees round the cottage, taking up the window light for certain.

Thomas paused for breath near the gate. Was he looking at the price of false evidence, or blackmail perhaps, or even murder?

"It *is* pretty, isn't it?" said a feminine voice from some
where near.

"Er—yes, indeed," responded Thomas, though he
couldn't see anyone at all.

"People often tell me I should have it painted when all
the roses are out over the door." The sound came from the
direction of a big yew.

"Rather difficult to get at the woodwork then," said
Thomas practically. "A pity to spoil the roses, too. I should
have it done in the spring."

"Not the house painted, a picture of the house painted."
The voice materialised into a spinster of about sixty. This
must be Miss Casterton. She had on an overall of flowered
cotton and big gardening gloves. "I've always meant to try
it myself, but somehow when you have a garden there
doesn't seem time for anything else."

"There's always something to be done in a garden,"
agreed Thomas, who rarely did anything in his.

"Always, but I don't like the winter when there's almost
nothing. I like to be out of doors." She peered vaguely
over the garden fence at Thomas. "Were you interested in
the cottage?"

Thomas told her exactly what had brought him there.

"Shambrook," she said. "Giles Shambrook. I can't say I
know the name. I bought the house through agents in
Calleford, but the owners hadn't a name like that or I
should have remembered it. I know about the Barbarys, of
course."

"You do?" responded Thomas eagerly.

"Well, I know they owned the Manor for donkeys' years
and were very good to the parish. In fact, I'm one of the
trustees of the Barbary almshouses." Miss Casterton
sighed audibly. "You don't get private generosity on that
scale these days, not with taxation what it is."

Thomas allowed a few moments of respectful silence to
elapse to the memory of the good old days, and then
returned to Giles Shambrook.

"I expect you'd like to see inside. It's not very tidy," she
warned him doubtfully. "I'm always out of doors, you see."

Thomas followed her into the cottage. It was dark and
crowded inside, with heavy Victorian furniture crammed

unsuitably into oak beamed rooms. Thomas could quite see why it was its owner preferred to spend her time in the garden.

"You won't want to see the attic," she said briskly, pointing to a narrow, twisting little stairway which led off the upstairs landing.

"No," agreed Thomas. It was just as well he felt no inclination to see the attic. The stairs were piled high with old gardening magazines. "It's a bit unusual to find an attic in a cottage like this, isn't it?"

"It's not very big really, just a room in one of the gables. I don't use it. Mind you I think this must have been more than just a cottage in the old days. More like a home farm . . ."

Thomas shook his head. "I doubt it. It would be nearer for one thing . . ."

"But that's just why. It's because it's so near, you see, that I wondered."

"Near? It's not near the Manor. I've walked up here past the church."

"Oh, but it is, Mr. Harding. If you go on walking instead of going back the way you came, you'll come out at the Manor. The path is a bit over-grown, but I dare say you can get through."

It took Thomas about a quarter of an hour to get back to the Manor by the path, but this was not because it was a long way. It was because the going was rough and he was thinking. At every turn he seemed to find something odd about Easterbrook. First of all there was the Barbary murder, with all its inconsistencies and mysteries, and then there was the murder of Mary Fenny and the flight of her husband with all *its* sinister implications—to say nothing of minor puzzles like the way in which Charlie Ford had disappeared this afternoon and the behaviour of Sammy the cat. He hadn't had time to work out just how Sammy had got indoors. There was just one thing to be said for the whole crazy situation. He hadn't been bored since the moment he began measuring up his own drawing-room.

Thomas paused to take in his surroundings. The path along which he was walking was broad and grass-lined with brambles growing wild across it and hawthorn along its edges. It was a curious way. He was near enough to the village street but could see no houses from where he walked. The old path wound its way towards the Manor in a broad curve from the church and The George, past Yew Tree Cottage. It ran along just under the brow of Medlar Rise, the gentle little hill that rose behind the village, and was distinctly lower than the surrounding fields.

He resumed his walk. He had needed that rest for he had travelled farther than usual today. As he carefully threaded his way through the undergrowth he tried to fit this old road into the picture of the Easterbrook of yesterday. Every now and then he came across a stile, so there was little doubt of its being a right of way. In the distance he could see some overhead electricity cables, otherwise he might well have been in another century.

He came up to the Manor suddenly and was literally on his own back door step almost before he realised it.

"So the Barbarys had their own private way to the church," he concluded to Dora. "I wonder why."

"It must have been the Barbarys, I suppose? Not the Cloakes? It sounds a very old road."

"They were Catholics. They wouldn't have wanted to go to church. At least not after the death of Mary."

That evening they had a visit from the Rector.

"Forgive my disturbing you both," began Mr. Martindale, "but I come on a parochial duty."

Thomas settled him in a chair and begged him to go on.

"It is in the matter of the Barbary Almshouses. You have, Mr. Harding, I know been interested in them for—um—various reasons. I don't suppose you would have known old Jenkins who was our treasurer for many years. He died last month and the office is now vacant. I've just come from the quarterly meeting of the trustees, and we feel that we could not have a better man than yourself as his successor." He addressed Thomas but he looked at Dora. "If you felt you could take it on, that is."

Thomas gave a self-deprecating little laugh. "You want a younger, more active man than me for a job like that, Rector. Someone still in touch with the financial world."

Mr. Martindale nodded. "Let me see now, Harold Jenkins was eighty-one, I think—or was it eighty-two?"

"How much work is involved?" asked Dora.

"Not much, Mrs. Harding. All the money is invested in Government Stock..."

"Government Stock!" ejaculated Thomas in spite of himself.

"Government Stock," said the Rector calmly, "so it's quite safe."

"Safe from what?"

"The income is not high," admitted the Rector, "but we do what we can with it."

"The cottages could do with bringing up to date," said Dora, "though I've only seen them from the outside."

"It's as much as we can do to maintain them," said the Rector sadly, "without thinking of modernising them. Charlie Ford is very good but we can't expect him to work for nothing."

"Couldn't you raise some capital and do it that way? It wouldn't make very much difference to your income but it would help the occupants a lot."

Mr. Martindale looked seriously at Dora.

"Mrs. Harding, you can see what a blessing your husband would be to the trustees and our pensioners..."

Thomas shook his head.

"There's the question of a grant from the local authority too," said the Rector, "but somehow I don't feel Miss Casterton and I are the right people to deal with the Rural District Council. We lack experience or skill or something. And then there are the Charity Commissioners. Speaking for myself I find the Ecclesiastical Commissioners take up a great deal of my time let alone their—er—brothers in Charity. Besides," said the Rector with a disarming twinkle, "there really isn't anyone else, is there?"

Ten

ONE of the by-products of the Barbary mystery so to speak was that Thomas no longer resented sitting down in the mornings. That hiatus which used to follow breakfast had gone. Instead he now walked firmly to the drawing-room, a man of purpose. That was not to say that he did something each morning but that he had something to do if he wanted to. He usually beat Gladys to the drawing-room by a short head.

"Is it all right for me to do in here, Mr. Harding?" Gladys went through the ritual of asking this every morning.

"Quite all right, Gladys." It was like responding to the Rector's bidding in church. Both would have been startled by any variation.

She moved her cloths and dusters over to the fireplace and began her daily stint on the panelling.

Thomas let her get started, then: "I went to see Yew Tree Cottage yesterday."

"Miss Casterton, the gardening lady," supplied Gladys.

"Gladys," he said curiously, "when they say 'Mr. Harding', what do they put after that?"

"The invalid gentleman," said Gladys without hesitation.

"And the Templeton-Smythe's, what did they call them?"

"I don't think anybody called them anything, Mr. Harding."

"A nice cottage Miss Casterton's got," said Thomas hastily. He might miss the double-talk, the quick-fire responses of the city but there was country wit too—slower and different, but there all right.

"Shouldn't like that cottage myself," said Gladys. "Too lonely up that road. Mother wouldn't like it either. Nothing goes by that way any longer."

"I noticed that," said Thomas. "I came back that way to the Manor yesterday. It's quite overgrown."

"That's right," said Gladys. "It's Henry Brown's job to keep that clear." She gave Thomas a meaning glance. "And he reckons nobody uses it anyhow so he don't trouble."

"Ah," said Thomas.

He watched Gladys's arms working like a flail on the panelling, up and down, across and back, tirelessly.

"That road," said Gladys presently. "Old Mrs. Meredith used to say it was a smugglers' road or something..."

"Did she?" said Thomas, interested.

"There was a poem she used to say a lot. She liked poetry but I never seemed to get on with it at school myself. I was better with the Bible somehow. Sort of easier to learn if you know what I mean." With which passing tribute to the Old Testament poets she shook her duster vigorously.

Thomas nodded a trifle absently, his mind on the road. A smugglers' road; that was a new thought.

"Because it was sunken or something," said Gladys.

He should have spotted that himself, thought Thomas. She was right. It was a sunken road, cut very low in the ground, with banks built up...

"You can tell there's something funny about it," said Gladys, "if you stand by Yew Tree Cottage. You'd think you ought to be able to see the village from there only you can't." She rubbed the skirting right down by the floor. "That's why Mother wouldn't like it."

He pictured it in his mind. "I know why that is, Gladys. That little hill on the left..."

"Medlar Rise."

"Medlar Rise, well it's because the road's been cut under the curve of the hill. Yes, I see it now. Mrs. Meredith was right. It could have been a smugglers' road. You see there wouldn't have been any silhouette on the skyline of anyone using the road, would there?"

Gladys stepped back and looked at the panelling.

"That's right, Mr. Harding."

Thomas sank back in his chair and deliberately evoked the image of smugglers riding by in the night with muffled traces and an anxious eye kept on the moon and the road behind. There would have been a fair bit of smuggling going on in these parts in the old days, he decided. Easterbrook, and Calleford, too, for that matter, were near enough to the coast to have seen "free-trading" in their time, and both lay between London and the sea. He had imagined it was a road from the Manor to the church...

"Of course that road goes to The George too, doesn't it," he said aloud, "as well as to the church."

"That's right, Mr. Harding. That's as far as Henry Brown gets. Keeps all the roads all right as far as The George does Henry Brown."

Thomas grinned. Next time he was in the village he would go in The George himself and ask the landlord if he had heard tell of smuggling.

Of course, it couldn't be anything to do with the Barbarys but it would be interesting...

Or could it be something to do with the Barbarys? He had heard smuggling of that sort went on right up to Napoleon's day, but could it have concerned people like the Barbarys? Surely Sir Toby Barbary would have been too well established to need to traffic in contraband? But... he was struck by a sudden thought. Sir Richard Barbary had in effect closed that smugglers' road when he was instrumental in building the new bridge lower down the river. Had that been coincidence? He must make a note about that, in case it mattered. Besides, he didn't like coincidences.

"Of course, Gladys," he said, "it's the obvious way for you to come to work, isn't it? If your friend Henry Brown were to clear—"

"Henry Brown's no friend of mine," said Gladys tartly.

"If the way were clear," amended Thomas, "then it would be much quicker than going round by the other road."

"Oh, I wouldn't come that way, Mr. Harding. It's not interesting at all."

He cast about in his mind for what it could be that was interesting between Gladys's cottage and the Manor.

There was the church, and the village shop and then the telephone kiosk, and the post office and Charlie Ford's builder's yard . . .

That sequence of thought stirred a memory somewhere. He paused, searching in his mind—but it was gone, faintly teasing from a distance. He waited a moment but the memory remained elusive. Perhaps if he thought about something else it would come back . . . especially if it was important.

It was important, he was sure. Memory had told him that much before it capriciously withdrew the recollection.

He sought for something to talk about to Gladys. The other would come back to him.

"What news of Alan Fenny now?"

"None, Mr. Harding. Nobody knows anything."

"I'll bet they don't," said Thomas to himself. Aloud he said, "Time's getting on, isn't it? I mean he must be somewhere, mustn't he?"

"That's right," contributed Gladys.

"Food and drink and shelter. He must have those, mustn't he? Somewhere."

"That's right," said Gladys. "But he hasn't been near his mother, that I do know."

"I'll bet he hasn't," said Thomas warmly. "But the police . . ."

"They're just waiting, Mr. Harding. They reckon if they wait he'll show himself in the end. 'Course they don't know for certain sure that he's still in the village, do they?"

"That's a point. He might have gone off again that day."

"That's right," said Gladys, taking a big sweep up to the top with her duster.

Thomas chuckled. "I thought for one moment that he might have made for my priest's hole here . . ."

Gladys's arm stopped halfway across her dusting arc.

"No, Gladys, don't worry. I realised afterwards he couldn't be in there because of your Charlie Ford screwing it up. No one's been in or out since that happened."

The polishing arm resumed its regular movements.

"But it was a nice thought, wasn't it? I mean, it's had

quite a history, that little room. It's used to fugitives, you might say."

"Alan wouldn't have known about that room anyway, Mr. Harding. He couldn't have, could he?"

"No," said Thomas comfortably. "I realised that myself. He was skipping about the countryside before any of us knew about the room."

It was very peaceful, sitting there watching Gladys rubbing away at the panelling. There was something very relaxing about... then it came back to him.

"I've got it," he said aloud.

"Got what, Mr. Harding?" Gladys stopped again, her dusting arm outstretched.

"I saw Mr. Ford, the builder, down by the church yesterday afternoon. I wanted to ask him something, but when I thought I'd caught up with him, he wasn't there. He must have come up this old road then."

"That's right," said Gladys, going back to her polishing.

"I'd wanted to ask him something that seemed important at the time, I remember... oh, yes, I know what it was... the priest's hole. He'd screwed it up because he didn't want anyone going inside it and..." Thomas stopped.

Put that way...

"Left some wires bare or something, hadn't he?" contributed Gladys. "Not what you could call a fast worker, cousin Charlie. Mind you, Mr. Harding, he's thorough, that you can say for him."

For Gladys that was a long speech. Thomas looked at her with interest.

"You wouldn't have seen him either, Mr. Harding, not if he'd nipped up the old road. You wouldn't see anyone, not that was coming this way by the old road..."

"No Gladys," said Thomas softly. "You wouldn't see anyone coming this way by the old road, would you?"

She bent diligently towards the skirting. He couldn't see her face now.

"They would be quite safe, Gladys, wouldn't they, coming this way from the church to the Manor? No one would see them, no one at all."

There was a flurry of a duster being shaken but no reply from Gladys.

"Just Miss Casterton," said Thomas speculatively. "That's all you'd have to keep an eye open for, eh, Gladys? Old Miss Casterton who's always bending over some flower or other . . ."

"I don't know what you mean, Mr. Harding."

"Don't you, Gladys? I wonder . . ."

How stupid he had been. A naïve, imperceptive fool, that's what he was. His brain was atrophying here in the country, going to seed, that's what was happening to him.

"Charlie Ford came here that way, didn't he, that day?"

"I'm sure I don't know, Mr. Harding. . . ."

"And he wasn't the only one to use that road, Gladys, was he?"

"Wasn't he, Mr. Harding?"

"No Gladys, he was not." Thomas kept in his chair with difficulty, but he must be careful, very careful now what he said and did. This could be very important, this might explain a lot of things, inexplicable things . . . like the cat that came in in the night.

"And your Charlie Ford comes along and starts a job and doesn't finish it, does he?"

"He often does that, Mr. Harding," offered Gladys. "Always getting called away, is our Charlie. You know what it is. Some people won't wait, you know . . ."

"So he leaves the wiring in a dangerous condition and screws up the hole so I don't go inside."

"He wouldn't like anyone to get hurt, Mr. Harding," said Gladys expressionlessly. "Ever so careful, he is."

"I agree with you there," conceded Thomas. Things were beginning to fit together. His pulse quickened. He thought he knew now where Charlie Ford had gone that day. He knew, too, how it was that Alan Fenny had slipped out of sight so easily too. And kept out of sight?

"Gladys," he said suddenly, "I think we shall have to ask your cousin Charlie to come round here and open up the panelling."

"Very well, Mr. Harding, though I'm sure he wouldn't have closed it up if he didn't think it was important."

Now what exactly did she mean by that? Thomas stared

at her back. Was she following his train of thought or wasn't she?

"There," she said, running the duster over the last bit of panelling. "Coming up ever so nice, isn't it? I'm finished in here for today unless there was anything else, Mr. Harding?"

"Nothing, thank you, Gladys. You've been a great help already."

She hadn't been out of the room more than a minute when Dora came hurrying in.

"Thomas, what's upset Gladys? She came straight through and said she must go home. And she went—just like that."

"I upset her."

"Thomas!"

"I did. Or to be accurate—my line of reasoning upset her."

"Not Gladys . . ."

"Wait till you hear what the reasoning was . . ."

When Dora heard she was adamant.

"You must send for the police, Thomas. It's the only thing to do. If Alan Fenny is in there . . ."

"It all seems to fit in—the old hidden road here, Charlie Ford screwing up the hole, Sammy getting in the house when he shouldn't, the fact that officially no one's seen Fenny and yet his mother knew I'd seen him . . ."

"Well, if he is and you open the hole in the panelling yourself what's going to happen? You might get hurt."

"I don't mind that but—"

"*I* do."

"But *you* might be injured, too. He'll be pretty desperate."

"He'll get away, of course," said Dora. "You and I couldn't stop a healthy young man."

"I couldn't trip up a babe in arms," admitted Thomas sadly. "Not now."

"And where would we be, I ask you, when he gets away?"

"Back where we started," agreed Thomas, "with old Mrs. Fenny still being watched by the police and her son wandering around determined to solve all his own problems himself. I suppose you're right. We must send for the police." He shook his head. "I don't like doing that somehow."

"What else can we do?"

"It'll be the end of us here, you realise that, don't you? We'll be outside for ever more."

"We're outsiders now," said Dora crisply. "And likely to be until we've lived here fifty years and more. However innocent Easterbrook thinks this young man is, do you think either of us is going to sleep comfortably in our beds tonight with the thought that he's probably hiding in our priest's hole?"

"A proper fool I shall look now if he isn't," said Thomas.

The police came willingly enough.

"Sounds quite a possibility," agreed Inspector Bream when he had heard Thomas propound his theory. "He could have got up here without being seen that day when Constable Wilkins here let him through his fingers."

"He'd never have seen him on that road," agreed Thomas.

P.c. Wilkins said nothing.

"And then," went on Bream, "it's just a question of tricking us into not looking here for him." He glared at the panelling. "Though if he *is* in here someone's been perverting the course of justice, haven't they?"

"Not if it leads to his arrest," Dora chipped in.

"He may not be in there, of course," said Thomas hastily, "but if it was good enough for a priest I reckon it should be good enough for your man." He tapped the panelling. "I'm not sure that I like doing this, Inspector. If I were a fit man, I'm not certain that I wouldn't have opened the hide up myself."

"Would you, sir?" said the Inspector ruminatively. "Well, I'm sure you've done the right thing in sending for us, not to mention that fact that it's your duty, sir, isn't it? We'll see no harm comes to Easterbrook's precious Alan Fenny if he didn't touch his wife. Now, what we want is a screw-driver . . ."

It didn't take long. Thomas watched the policeman at

work with mixed feelings. It was a violation of his priest's hole, that was what it was.

"Now," said Bream, "if you and Mrs. Harding would stand back . . . where's the woman who works here, by the way?"

"Gladys? She's gone home."

Under the eagle eye of the Inspector, P.c. Wilkins undid the last screw and stepped back.

"Come on, come on then," snapped the Inspector impatiently. "You know how to open it."

Wilkins pushed the panel open and poked his torch inside.

The priest's hole was quite empty.

On the other hand there were no bare electrical wires in sight either. None whatsoever.

Eleven

IT was a chastened Thomas who came down to breakfast the next morning, after an indifferent night's sleep.

"Gladys?"

"Back," said Dora, "but very quiet."

He and Dora had said very little after the police had gone, and it was quite a relief to him to find a letter from Mr. Archibald Mellon in his post.

"We are to have a visitor, dear."

"Nice or nasty?"

"The Honorary Secretary of the Calleshire County Archaeological and Historical Society, to wit Mr. Archibald Mellon."

"Ah," said Dora non-committally.

"Nice, I should think," said Thomas. "There's something quite attractive to me already about history, and a mystery where all the participants have been dead and gone these hundred years and more seems positively simple."

"Don't be bitter, dear."

"Well, I've never felt such a—"

"When's he coming?" asked Dora swiftly. "This Mr. Mellon?"

Thomas turned the letter over. "He will wait upon me at eleven o'clock in the forenoon and begs to remain my obedient servant."

Thomas was therefore half prepared for the trim little figure with a goatee beard whom Gladys announced on the stroke of eleven.

What he wasn't prepared for was Mr. Mellon's enthusiasm.

"My dear sir, a real find, a very real find indeed. A new

107

priest's hole. So many of them were walled up or taken down. We must get in touch with the Catholic Record Society straightaway. Now, then, where exactly is it?"

Thomas led the way to the panelling.

"A hole in the wall!" exclaimed Mellon. "Very rare that for a priest's hole. First thing the pursuivants would do would be to tap that panelling. Give the game away at once. Probably not genuine."

"I'm sure it's genuine," retorted Thomas, a trifle stiffly. "A Catholic family called Cloake lived here and they were imprisoned for Popish practices, and if that didn't mean they sheltered a priest here then I don't know what it did mean."

"Attended Mass, I expect," said Mellon absently. He was examining the woodwork closely. "This is Tudor panelling all right."

Thomas was indignant. "I should say so. The whole house is Tudor."

The little man frowned. "Not quite. The windows of the room above this are Georgian. About 1800, I should say."

"1780," admitted Thomas, remembering the book in the Calleford Library.

"Hrrmph. Now, you say that your priest's hole is behind this panelling. Don't tell me where. Let me try and find the entrance myself. It tells me what sort of chance the poor blighter inside had of being caught."

He began to tap the wall all over, listening carefully for a difference in the sound. He didn't stop talking.

"Most of these priest's holes were hidden in chimney shafts, or under false fireplaces. Hides they were called. Sometimes they converted an old garderobe or sewer or got into an attic gable. There's one very clever one behind a cupboard. All the shelves tip back and there's your hide behind that. Easy to feed your priest that way too. Just put your food in the cupboard and close the door. He does the rest. Mind you, the pursuivants were clever too. Sat and waited for days if necessary—like a cat watching for a mouse to come out. Hunger did the trick quite often, and treachery. This panelling sounds the same all over to me."

"It is," murmured Thomas. "It's the same thickness all its length. So your pursuivants could tap it all day long and 't would sound the same. Moreover, they could go into the study and tap there and they would get exactly the same sound."

"But they would be tapping two different walls not different sides of the same piece of wood." He nodded. "Clever, very clever."

He stepped backwards and took a good look at the wall.

"You'd never guess, would you," said Thomas.

"Never, my dear sir, never. But I haven't found the way n yet."

Thomas put his hands on the secret panel and swung it open.

Archibald Mellon rubbed his hands together briskly.

"Capital. Yes, I'm prepared to agree this was built for a recusant priest to hide in. The date is about right and the fact that the family were imprisoned really is more than suggestive that they were caught at something."

"One thing puzzles me," said Thomas. "Was this hide built when this house was put up?"

Mellon shook his head. "Most unlikely. You can't keep a secret from your builders, and you know how everyone takes a good look at a house under construction. They would do that just as much then as now. When did your Cloake family sell up?"

"1587. That's when the Barbarys came."

"This house is older than that. In any case these hides were almost always built in afterwards. Skilled job, too." Mellon stuck his head through the hole in the panelling. "Shall I lead the way in?"

After he had explored the hide the historian made for the chimney. There wasn't room for both of them there so Thomas took the opportunity of sitting down. When Dora came into the room some minutes later she was rewarded with the sight of a pair of well-trousered legs standing in the fireplace. Some rather muffled sounds reached them both.

"Our visitor has arrived," Thomas informed her.

"By reindeer?"

Thomas glanced out of the window. "By car, alas."

"It's a funny noise in there."

"That is Mr. Archibald Mellon still talking. He knows

his stuff though. If you go a bit nearer you will doubtless be able to hear what he is saying."

Dora advanced to the fireplace and listened to the words which came floating down the chimney.

"There's probably an air vent from your hide into this chimney if we knew where to look. I can't get quite high enough. I shall need something to stand on and a torch."

"I'll get them for you," said Dora.

At the sound of her voice Archibald Mellon withdrew from the fireplace and executed a courtly bow, redolent of an earlier, more gracious age. Thomas introduced them briefly.

"Allow me to congratulate you, Mrs. Harding, on having such an interesting as well as charming drawing-room."

"It is a genuine priest's hole, then?"

"Undoubtedly. There really are no reservations about it in my mind, and when we find the chapel we can be absolutely certain."

"Find the chapel?" echoed Thomas.

"But of course. That was why you hid a priest in your house in the first place—so that he could say Mass. If you had a lot of Catholics round and about, you had secret signals telling them when the service was to be held. In one place laying out a sheet on a certain hedge would tell those people in the know. That was the whole point in sheltering a priest. They used to travel the country saying Mass."

"But we haven't a chapel here in the Manor," said Dora.

"You don't know of one," he corrected her. "There must have been one somewhere about. Of course they could have had one of those movable altars which could be closed, and used chalices that unscrewed and so forth— but mostly there would be a place where Mass could be said."

Thomas looked at Dora who said weakly, "You'd better stay for luncheon, Mr. Mellon."

Archibald Mellon stayed for luncheon, and he stayed for tea and he searched the house. He and Thomas spent a good hour up in the attics, clambering about among the chimney stacks but discovered no sign of a chapel.

"It is usual to find the chapel in the attic," panted

Mellon, as he squeezed past the main chimney breast, "but really, Harding, your attics are uncommonly dull."

"I'm sorry," apologised Thomas drily. "I would have preferred a house without any. Why did they choose the attics?"

"Furthest place from the front door as a rule. Gave them time to hide if the priest hunters arrived. And the right shape, too, though I doubt if that had much to do with it."

"Any priest would have had to go towards the pursuivants though," objected Thomas, "from these attics to get to the hide in this house."

Mellon tugged at his beard. "That's a very good point. But I am quite sure with a well-built hide like that in the house there must have been a chapel somewhere. That secret room wasn't built for a priest just passing through."

They finished up together in the drawing-room in the late afternoon, Thomas more tired than he had been for months.

"Of course, there'll be documentary evidence," said the indefatigable Mellon. "I'll start looking for that in the morning."

"There's one book which probably had a good description of the hide in it." And Thomas told him about the family history, and its two missing pages. "The last words on the previous page were: 'The Manor was a well known Catholic one, ideal for the purpose of secret worship on account of its secluded position in a small village. I have been unable to find out who built it but the handiwork of Nicholas . . .' That's where the pages were gone. I don't know if it helps at all."

"If it helps! My dear sir, it makes all the difference." Mr. Mellon jumped out of his chair and began pacing the room excitedly. " 'The handiwork of Nicholas'—that will be Nicholas Owen. He built many of these hides, and built them better than anyone else."

"That's a historical fact, is it?" asked Thomas, anxious to be clear on this.

"Definitely. He would come to the house as a servant and work as one during the day, and then at night he would make a hide, like this one of yours, and no one but the priest and the owner would be any the wiser."

"He must have been an excellent craftsman," put in Dora.

"He was indeed, Mrs. Harding. He preferred to work in stone but he—if it was he—has made a good job of this one in wood. He thought up the most ingenious hides—in false chimney stacks and underneath staircases, even building floors at different levels."

"Was he a priest then?"

"No, only a lay brother. He was a servant to one, Father Garnet, a Jesuit. They called him Little John and sometimes Little Michael, for, of course, they all ran a perpetual risk of being caught, but his real name was Nicholas Owen." Mellon pointed to the panelling. "This won't be the last of his hides to be found either. No one knows how many he built or where he built them because he never talked. And he made a habit of never building two hides in the same manner so that the finding of one in one house wouldn't lead to the finding of a similar hide in another. Many a Jesuit priest owed his life to Nicholas Owen."

Thomas stirred. "I should like to know whether one ever sheltered here."

"My dear sir, you can be sure of it. If Nicholas Owen built this—and it looks to me very much as if he did—then some priest was either living in or calling regularly at the house to say Mass and was likely to be sought for here by the pursuivants."

"And could have been caught here by them in 1587?"

"Very probably. From what you say, the Cloakes had been penalised pretty heavily, and priest-harbouring was just about the worst crime in that particular calendar."

There was a little silence while Dora filled their teacups and Thomas wondered how it was he once thought Easterbrook Manor lacked the right atmosphere. He certainly wouldn't want to live anywhere else now.

"How does one go about finding out if a priest was caught here, and who he was?" asked Thomas at length.

"Recusant Rolls of the Exchequer after 1592, Pipe Rolls before. And the Catholic Record Society of course." Mr. Mellon put down his cup and saucer and for the first time that day spoke diffidently. "Mr. Harding, were you planning to publish anything about this hide?"

Thomas shook his head. "I don't know enough history to publish anything."

"Then might I? The Chronicles of our Society—"

"Of course," said Thomas warmly. "I shall be delighted if you would find out all you can about the Cloakes and the hide. My real interest you know is in a skeleton I found in the hide, a victim of murder."

"Elizabethan?" Mellon leant forward eagerly.

"Put there in 1815."

The historian sank back in his chair. "Not my period at all. You'll have to write that up yourself, Mr. Harding, for our Chronicles, you know."

"Mr. Mellon," said Dora swiftly, "what happened to Nicholas Owen in the end?"

He turned to Dora. "He was caught and tortured to death in the Tower of London. At least," qualified the historian, with a commendable regard for the exact truth, "the Lieutenant of the Tower at the time reported, 'The man is dead, he died on our hands.' He didn't talk, even then, you see."

"Poor man," said Dora compassionately.

"They were hard times for any non-conformist," agreed Mellon. "The Catholic Church beatified Owen much later."

"I've never even liked going round the Tower," said Dora. "History always seems such an unhappy business."

Both men regarded this feminine sentiment as unworthy of notice, and Archibald Mellon began a further rumination about Nicholas Owen.

"There was one very interesting feature of his work, you know. As a rule when he built a hide he would build another exit to it, if possible to another bolt hole. The idea was that if the searchers found the hide empty they would go away when in fact the priest had retreated to an even smaller space behind the hide." He looked across at Thomas. "If we could find a bolt hole from your hide it would be almost conclusive proof that Nicholas Owen built it."

"That will have to wait until another day, I'm afraid, Mr.

Mellon," said Dora briskly. "My husband is an invalid, you know."

"I did do some measurements of the upstairs rooms in the beginning," said Thomas slowly, "but the police took them away. They would be worth doing again. A bolt hole like that would take up very little space."

Dora was adamant. "Not today."

"Tomorrow?" suggested Archibald Mellon optimistically.

So it was settled that the historian should return the next morning and that he and Thomas would do some accurate measuring to see if Nicholas Owen had built a bolt hole beyond the hide, and that Mellon should take some photographs for his article.

"We might have another look for a chapel," said Mellon hopefully as he took his leave. "I still can't understand why we can't find it."

But Archibald Mellon was not to revisit the Manor for some time. Thomas was quite exhausted by his energetic visitor, and their extensive scramblings over the Manor; and though he wouldn't have admitted it for worlds he felt the effects of having missed his afternoon rest. He went gladly to bed that night a very tired man.

At two o'clock in the morning he was a very ill man.

Dr. Curzan was summoned by a worried Dora as Thomas lay as still as he could, his face an ashen grey.

"I'm sorry, Doctor," he gasped painfully.

Dr. Curzan smiled, his daytime briskness forgotten. "You want a good sleep and a few days in bed. Been over-doing it, I expect."

He slid a needle expertly into Thomas's arm.

"I did have rather a heavy day," admitted Thomas, and then he fell thankfully to sleep away from the pain in his chest.

The doctor came again the next morning and was reassuring but firm. The Rector came too and was gentle and kind. Gladys came to do his room and was concerned and not a little overawed at his illness.

"You all right, Mr. Harding?" she enquired anxiously. "It won't worry you if I do in here?"

"I'm fine, Gladys," he said weakly.

"Mr. Harding, did that man with the beard find anything yesterday?"

"Mr. Mellon? No, not really. He knows all about Elizabethan hiding places though. He's going to write an article about it."

Gladys seemed suitably impressed by this and applied herself to cleaning the bedroom. Thomas was dozing by the time she left.

He spent much of that and the following day asleep and then began to feel better. And as soon as he felt better he found being in bed irksome.

"Another day or so," decreed Dr. Curzan during a brief visit on Monday morning. "You're doing very nicely. You don't want to spoil it by getting up too soon. Besides you must be well enough for the village hall concert. Can't have you missing that."

Thomas bowed to this reluctantly. There were so many things to be done if the murderer of young Toby Barbary was ever to be found. He must find out more about this character, Giles Shambrook, and go back to the Calleford Public Library to consult the Baronetage. He wanted to read the obituary of Sir Richard, the 9th Baronet, too, in the Calleford *Courier* for 1835.

He wanted the ebullient Archibald Mellon to come back as well. What he had said about a chapel and a bolt hole made good sense. He lay on his bed staring at the ceiling. Was there a chapel hidden in the house, too? The beams of the ceiling contrasted oddly with the eighteenth-century windows. Had the Manor any more secrets to disclose?

He turned over uneasily. There was the other murder too. He couldn't forget that. Alan Fenny was still at large and looking for his wife's murderer. His mother knew that and knew where he was hiding. Thomas closed his eyes and trusted that for her own sake Mrs. Fenny didn't know the name of the murderer. He hoped, too, that the police were still keeping a constant watch on her cottage. That was her only safeguard from a murderer who knew why Alan had gone to ground. Thomas twisted his lips into a smile. It was ironic that Mrs. Fenny was protected by the police hope of catching her son.

There were other things to think about as he lay in his room; most worrying of all to Thomas had been his latest heart attack. What use to the world was a man of fifty-two who couldn't do without his afternoon rest?

After two days of this sort of cogitation Thomas was in very low spirits. He felt he would never get any nearer to solving any mystery lying here. As it happened he was wrong. The next clue to the Barbary murder was literally dropped into his lap as he lay in bed.

The Rector had come in to see Thomas most days, had a little chat and gone on his way. This time he came and stayed.

"We had an official meeting of the Trustees of the Barbary Almshouses last night," he began, drawing up a chair to the bedside. "You were unanimously elected treasurer."

Thomas tried to look interested. He had almost forgotten about the charity.

"The money is nominally invested in the names of myself and the Churchwardens but all the Trustees have a say in its disposal. We—ahem—never lack suggestions as to how it should be spent, but I fancy that you will be able to advise us on the wisest way."

Thomas watched passively as the Rector deposited a large bundle of books and papers on the eiderdown.

"These are the things old Jenkins left behind. Account books and so forth. You won't find the writing difficult to read—he wrote an excellent copperplate script—but I can't answer for the figures. Anyway, have a look at them and let me know."

"I don't know if the doctor would allow it yet." Thomas picked up a sheaf of papers in a desultory manner.

"I asked him," said the Rector simply, "and he said you were fit for the stiffest brainwork there was but you weren't to get out of bed until he saw you."

Thomas brightened at this. So he wasn't quite useless after all. When the Rector had gone he tackled the almshouses accounts with something of his old mental vigour. Soon he was doing the sort of lightning calculation that had led him to prosperity in business in London. At the end of an hour his brain was full of schemes for raising

money with which to modernize the old almshouses. The
Charity capital would have to be re-invested. That was
quite clear. Government Stock might have been just the
thing in 1816 and even in old Jenkins's day, but not now.
He wondered how tightly the capital was tied up, and
mentally drafted a letter to Puckle, Puckle and Nunnery.
They could advise him on how and where Charity capital
could be best invested. And then there was this question
of an Improvement Grant. He would bring that up at their
first meeting.

By the end of the day Thomas was positively cheerful.
He had mastered the late honorary treasurer's peculiar
system of keeping the accounts, and it only remained to
study the original deed by which the almshouses had been
founded to see what powers were vested in the Trustees.
He stretched himself more comfortably in bed and began
to read. One of the few advantages of illness was that it
freed one from the interruption of polite society.

Thomas had begun to relax among the innumerable
legal whereas's and heretofore's of the instrument when
his attention was caught by a subordinate clause. He read
it again to be sure. There was no doubt about it. The
donor of these six almshouses, Sir Richard Barbary, reserved unto himself the right to nominate the tenants in
his lifetime. Thomas adjusted a stray pillow thoughtfully.
There was probably nothing out of the ordinary in that,
when you came to think about it. It was no doubt the need
of one or two particular people that had prompted the gift
in the first place.

He reached out to the pile of books the rector had
brought. Somewhere was one recording the tenants. It
was stout and leatherbound, and though it had been
begun in 1816 it was nowhere near full. Thomas turned
back its pages. He would see who it was Sir Richard had
chosen for his almshouses.

Of the first six tenants, five had been servants at the
Manor.

"They can't all have been pensionable at exactly the
same moment," agreed Dora, when she brought up his
supper tray.

"Would five servants have been all they would have in a

house this size?" asked her husband humbly. "I know you
and Gladys manage wonderfully."

Dora tried to visualise unlimited housework being done
by unlimited servants—and failed. "Five ought to have
been enough," she said doubtfully, "but then there would
have been coachmen, I suppose, and gardeners."

"Somehow I don't think any of these five were outdoor
servants."

Something in his tone made Dora look up.

"I think," said Thomas, "they were packed off to those
almshouses to get them out of the house while the body of
Toby Barbary was put into that old priest's hide and the
drawing room walls plastered over."

She straightened the eiderdown automatically, saying
"And his new servants wouldn't know there was any wood
behind the plaster."

"Or that there was a room behind the wood."

Twelve

Dr. Curzan allowed Thomas out of bed a week after his heart attack.

"And when can I go out?" demanded Thomas in the fretful manner of a convalescent.

The doctor twisted his stethoscope into a figure of eight and stuffed it into his pocket.

"Saturday. Saturday evening, I think, don't you? Can't have any absentees from the village hall concert." He looked quizzically at Thomas. "I don't *think* the excitement will be too much for your heart, but if you feel ill after the soprano I shall quite understand."

Thomas had forgotten the significance of Saturday evening.

"So you've got a hand in the village hall, have you, Doctor? Don't tell me your funds are in Government Stock too?"

"Funds?" said Dr. Curzan breezily. "We haven't got any funds—just an overdraft. We're having this concert to keep the bank at bay until we have our Christmas pantomime." He grinned. "On second thoughts, Mr. Harding, if you could feel ill *during* the soprano it would be better."

Thomas looked up. "Then we could both come out."

Because of Thomas's illness Dora had missed her visit to Calleford the previous week. Next day she decided she must go alone.

"I shall be all right," Thomas assured her a dozen times.

"I must go," she said doubtfully, "but I don't like leaving you."

"I shall be quite all right," said Thomas patiently.

Dora took no notice. "Gladys will be here until twelve and I'll be back by one."

"Nothing much can happen in an hour," he said reasonably.

But it did.

He was sitting quietly in the drawing-room after Gladys had gone when the front door bell rang. He was feeling perfectly well and so went unhurriedly to answer it. On the step stood a lanky youth somewhere about the age of twenty-one or twenty-two with the sort of close-cropped haircut Thomas associated with prisons and the Army.

"Good morning?" said Thomas interrogatively. There was something unusual about the young man's clothes too. He was wearing a brown suit with a collar that was almost rolled.

"Mr. Thomas E. Harding?"

"Yes," admitted Thomas warily. He couldn't place the boy's accent either.

"I thought the best thing to do was to come."

Thomas eyed him cautiously. He had never seen him before. There was a certain tautness in his manner though which interested him.

"I don't think I know you," began Thomas.

The youth set down the leather grip he was carrying and smiled rather solemnly. "Sure, you don't know me, Mr. Harding. You've never seen me before. Barbary's the name. You wrote me—remember? Thaddeus Barbary from Detroit. Mostly I'm called Tad."

"Bless my soul," ejaculated Thomas. It was an expression he almost never used. "Come in."

Tad Barbary picked up his grip and stepped into the home of his ancestors.

"You wrote me a letter. I thought the best thing to do was to come," he said again.

"Yes, indeed. Come in and sit down." Thomas led the way to the drawing-room and thankfully sank into his chair. "I'm delighted to be the first to welcome you back to Easterbrook."

The young man grinned. He had a pleasant face when he relaxed.

"You weren't quite the first, Mr. Harding. I asked a man the way here and he said to tell you Charlie Ford had got them switches and would be up next week."

"Those," said Thomas automatically.

"I thought it might be," agreed the young man gravely, "but as I was in Rome . . ."

Thomas pointed to the panelling indignantly. "Charlie Ford kept me out of that secret room there that I wrote to you about by a trick. I want to see him pretty badly."

"A trick that worked?"

"Until we had a look in there in spite of him," growled Thomas. "But that wasn't for a whole week."

"A whole week?" drawled the young man from Detroit. The smile had gone from his face and was in his voice now.

Thomas laughed. "You have no idea how attached I have become to my priest's hole."

"You found it yourself?" suggested Tad.

But Thomas needed no prompting to tell his story.

The young man sat and listened in silence and then went with him to the hide. Thomas could tell nothing from his face.

"What really is magnificent," said Thomas, back in his chair, "is to have a Barbary back in Easterbrook after all these years." He peered across at his guest. "Let me see, it must be over ninety years since Sir Walter died. He would have been your—ah—great, great, great-uncle, wouldn't he?"

"Sounds pretty far back," agreed Tad.

"Not so very far in the history of your family."

Tad bowed his head. "It's just that all those 'greats' make it seem that way." He waved a hand round the room. "Perhaps it's easier when there's something like this to remind you."

A door thudded in the background. "Thomas, I'm back."

Dora surged into the drawing-room hung about with parcels. Both men rose to their feet, Thomas clearing his throat ceremoniously.

"Dora, my dear, we have a guest. May I introduce Sir Thaddeus Barbary of Easterbrook."

Tad solemnly freed her of two of her parcels before she could shake his hand.

"Mostly I'm called Tad," he said again.

"But you're in America," protested Dora. "My husband wrote you there. Detroit, wasn't it?"

"Detroit, it was," agreed Tad. "When I had his letter decided to come."

"Then you have something to tell my husband?"

"Something to ask him, Mrs. Harding."

But Dora would not let them go on from there. The ebullient Archibald Mellon was too prominent in her memory. She insisted on a quiet conversational luncheon about the present not the past.

Tad gave her a tight smile. "Where I come from no one considers that the past could be more exciting than the right now. The present, yes, and the future always. But I don't go along with that myself. I've read some English history and that's not dull."

Dora crumbled some bread between her fingers and said delicately, "Tell me, Sir Thaddeus, do you do anything?"

Tad looked mystified. "Lots of things, Mrs. Harding."

"For a living," supplemented Thomas.

"Oh, work! Sure. I work for a guy in Detroit who's a realtor. At least I did until last week and now I don't any longer. I mustn't complain about him—he helped me raise my fare here. I had a go in an automobile factory for a bit and before that I was on the railroad." He must have caught sight of glances exchanged between Thomas and Dora because he went on quickly: "They didn't know about the title. Nobody did. I never used it after—after my father died."

Dora nodded comfortably. "Besides the Americans don't feel the same about titles as we do, do they? I never thought though that my husband and I should be the means of welcoming the Barbarys back to Easterbrook but I suppose it was bound to happen one day. Curiosity would bring you back in the end."

Thomas let Dora talk on while he took a good look at the fifteenth baronet. He gave the impression of a tightly coiled spring, held rigidly in check. He was spare in build, with a certain tense litheness about him that Thomas recognised. Here was a young man of awareness, one who had had to fend for himself in life.

"When did your father die?" he asked presently.

"Last year. He had been ill for a long time."

"And your mother? Is she still alive?" enquired Dora, taking his empty plate.

"No. She died when I was twelve." Tad deliberately took a long drink of water and Thomas changed the subject. Sir Thaddeus, too, would need time to settle down.

It was evening before they really got down to the Barbary family history. Thomas, rested and refreshed, collected his notebooks and sat himself in his armchair in the drawing-room. Dora got out her embroidery and sat opposite him.

"It's just as I imagined it," said Tad unexpectedly.

"Didn't you have any pictures?" asked Dora.

"No pictures, no drawings, nothing to tell me about Easterbrook, Mrs. Harding."

"There must be a reason for that."

"There was a reason," said Tad, "but I never got to know what it was. That's why I've come to England." He paused. "When my father died I found just one document among his things. That was a deed breaking something called the entail on this property."

Thomas nodded. "That's right. It was the only way they could sell the Manor."

"It was signed by two people—Theodore and Eugene Barbary. My father was Eugene's grandson. He used to tell people he was Sir Waldo Barbary and they used to laugh at him." He looked straightly at Thomas. "He was an alcoholic, you see, and they thought he was making it up."

"So he never really used his title," said Thomas reflectively.

"Sure he used it but nobody else did," Tad gave a short laugh. "They would say 'And I'm Napoleon'. I came not to believe in it myself."

"Money must come into this," said Thomas briskly. In his experience it usually did. "What happened to the money Theodore and Eugene got for the Manor and the land?"

"That went Las Vegas way. So did Theodore. I guess I could never make out just what happened to him but he didn't die from natural causes. Eugene was shot in a tavern brawl in 1908. His son died of drink and my father

caught the habit from him." He smiled tightly. "If the
family fortunes hadn't gone at Las Vegas I guess they
would have gone down one throat or another."

"But not yours," interposed Dora gently.

Tad looked disconcerted. "I guess not, Mrs. Harding,
but there's time yet. My mother used to say that there was
bad blood in the Barbarys."

Dora considered her silks against the light.

"I'm sure that's not so, Sir Thaddeus."

"It wasn't only my mother who thought that, Mrs.
Harding. My father knew it, too. There was something in
their past which they were afraid of, something in
England. Often I'd ask him about coming over here and
seeing the place, and he would look at me and say that we
could never come back."

A silence fell upon the little group in the drawing-room.
It was broken by Dora.

"Then I think it was very brave of you to do it."

Tad smiled but it was Thomas who spoke.

"This is all very interesting, you know. You turn up with
all the evidence of inherited feelings of guilt and here I
have the evidence of the crime—a hundred and fifty years
and over two thousand miles apart."

"It was certainly a legend that stuck in my father's
mind," said Tad. "I don't think he knew much more than
that his forebears had some good reason for not coming
back to England. Towards the end it was difficult to know
how much to believe. He was absolutely certain though
that the Barbarys would never prosper." He twisted his
lips ruefully. "It was difficult to argue the point with him
in view of the evidence."

"And yet neither your father nor Theodore nor Eugene
had anything to do with the crime." Thomas flipped back
the pages of his notebook. "You can be sure of that.
Theodore and Eugene probably knew about it, but it had
been committed before they were born. It was Theodore's
father Bertram who took at least the knowledge that the
murder had been done with him to America."

Tad nodded intelligently. "That was the man you wrote
me about."

"I wanted to know exactly when he went to the States."

"I can't tell you the month but I found out the year."

Thomas sat forward eagerly in his chair, Dora's needle was poised above her work.

Tad grinned. "It was an easy one to remember because you people had a big battle that year. 1815."

"Just as I thought," said Thomas quietly.

"The year of the murder?"

"Beyond any doubt."

"So great, great, great-grandfather Bertram ran away," said Tad thoughtfully. "He sure must have had a load on his conscience—though it wasn't fashionable to murder your nephew as late as the nineteenth century."

"I'm not sure if Bertram did murder young Toby, though I'm certain from what you say thàt he knew about the murder."

"You have another candidate?"

"The ninth baronet, his brother Richard."

"But he didn't run away."

"He didn't need to—not when Toby's father was killed in that battle you mentioned."

"All he needed was the nerve to stay put and step into the title and property," said Tad perceptively.

"Just that."

"But you have reasons too?"

Thomas beamed at him approvingly. "Good ones. Toby Barbary was supposed to have fallen in the river and drowned. The newspaper reports a witness who said he saw him fishing that afternoon." Thomas paused a trifle dramatically. "Sir Richard gave that witness a cottage."

Tad lifted his eyebrows. "Hush money?"

"That isn't all. Sir Richard—the good Sir Richard—gave the village six almshouses, remembering to reserve unto himself the right to nominate the occupants. Five of the first six were servants from the Manor, and they went into the almshouses in 1816."

"My husband thinks that was when that wall was plastered over," supplemented Dora. "Sir Richard would need to get the servants out of the way to do that if they knew about the priest's hole."

"What happened to—er—Toby's mother?"

"I don't know," confessed Thomas, "and I can't find out. She isn't buried here, but then there was nothing to keep her here after her husband and son were killed. She wouldn't have wanted to live on in this house with her brother-in-law. I think Sir Richard kept that body somewhere until she went and then brought it here."

"Why didn't he just bury it somewhere in the village?"

"I've thought about that quite a bit. He didn't push Toby in the river because his body would have fetched up in the mill dam about a quarter of a mile downstream, and his fractured skull would have been noticed. The fact that he was supposed to have been drowned and wasn't found in the mill dam was in itself suspicious. So suspicious that any new grave or even digging activity on the part of either Sir Richard or his confederates would have been immediately suspect."

"Not wise," agreed Tad. "He had the body and he had the ideal hiding place, but it was probably some time before he could bring the two together."

"Don't forget that the boy's father was still alive at the time of the murder. First of all he had to reckon on his coming home so the body wouldn't have been brought to the Manor first."

"His death must have been a stroke of luck for the murderer."

"Yes, but only that. It's one of the things that doesn't fit in at all," admitted Thomas. "We still don't know why the boy should have been killed and that is really the most important question of all. Somehow I have the feeling that Toby's father's death was a help but that it wasn't really significant."

Tad passed his hand through his close-cropped hair. "So Richard and Bertram murdered him but couldn't push his body in the river and couldn't bury it. Right?"

"Right. I think."

"So they had to hide it somewhere. Right?"

"Right," smiled Thomas.

Tad poled a finger towards the priest's hole.

"Why not there?"

"Too risky. The boy's mother was presumably still living here and his father and probably the servants knew all about the priest's hide. But after Waterloo, when Sir Richard inherited, things would be very different. Sir

Toby's widow almost certainly left, don't you think?" He turned to Dora. "I don't think any widow would stay on here with her brother-in-law, do you?"

"Not if she could help it, dear, especially if she had just lost her only son."

"Unless the whole thing turned her mind," suggested Tad.

"That's a point," said Thomas.

"I think," said Dora slowly, "that if she had a family anywhere she would have gone back to them."

Thomas nodded. "Perhaps we ought to slip over to Staplegate to see if she's there."

"Still?" Tad looked mystified.

"In the churchyard."

"Oh, I see."

"Where was I?" asked Thomas.

"Waterloo."

"Ah, yes. After Waterloo Sir Richard inherited, Sir Toby's widow left, there was no risk of Toby's father returning and Sir Richard was in charge of everything."

"This Sir Richard seems to have had it all his own way, doesn't he?" said Tad. "Getting away with murder, you might say."

"He went about it very carefully. First of all he destroyed all mention of the priest's hide in the family history his brother had written—you must read that, by the way—then he emptied his house of everyone who knew about the hide. Only then did he plaster over that panelling. He did the wall the other side of the fireplace too at the same time. Anyone who noticed the difference could be told it was to improve the appearance of the room."

"He was still pretty lucky, I guess," drawled Tad. "The boy's father is conveniently killed, his mother goes away and 'four-greats' grandfather Bertram goes to America for good."

"If you can kill your nephew, a brother wouldn't count for much," agreed Thomas.

Tad frowned. "What became of the other guy who was in on the murder, the one who was given the cottage?"

"That's a good point. We must find out when Giles Shambrook died, and how."

"And how," echoed Tad, with an exaggerated American accent and a perfectly straight face.

At ten o'clock Tad stood up and enquired the way to the nearest hotel, but he got no farther that night than the second best bedroom in Easterbrook Manor.

"We shall be delighted," insisted Thomas.

Next morning Dora took Thomas his breakfast in bed. Half an hour later she went up again with his post.

"What's he doing?" Thomas wanted to know.

"If you are referring to the fifteenth baronet," said Dora, "he's walking round and round the outside of the house murmuring 'Sir Thaddeus Barbary of Easterbrook' to himself in a rather dazed way."

"He's only a boy really," said Thomas. "Perhaps he'll look in and see me later on. There are one or two things I've thought about since last night."

"There are, are there?" said Dora drily. "You won't forget to save some of your strength for the concert, will you? We may both need it."

Thirteen

Tad's real introduction to England came, he declared for ever afterwards, at the village concert.

It was a new experience for Thomas and Dora too. They set off together after an early supper, Dora somewhat perplexed about what to wear.

"Gladys said something thin," she murmured, shivering a little as they stepped out of doors, "because they never open the windows."

"What, never?" said Thomas.

"According to Gladys 'only come Spring cleaning'," said Dora. She stopped. "Which way shall we go?"

"The sunken road," said Thomas, "while there's still enough light to show Tad Yew Tree Cottage." He stepped through the gate. "Besides it really is a quick way to the village."

All three of them halted in front of the half-timbered building. It looked different with the sun off it, much older and darker, with the old yews clustering round it protectively.

"That's what I call old," exclaimed Tad. "Real old."

"As old as the Manor anyway," said Thomas.

"Now if only that was standing in Detroit . . . Why, if that realtor I worked for there had that cottage for sale I do believe he could just name his figure."

The others laughed.

"What price the Manor then?" said Thomas.

"Priceless," said Tad seriously. "It's quite lovely. Bertram must have been out of his mind to leave it."

"I think he must," agreed Thomas. "I think he was out of his mind with worry, fear and guilt, and, to do him justice, remorse too."

129

"I guess that much has come down to me," said Tad. "Something, anyway, that said there was a nigger in the family woodpile."

"Imagine having to live on in the same house as your recently widowed sister-in-law when you've probably had a hand in killing her only son."

Tad shuddered. "Takes a bit of doing."

"I don't think Bertram was up to it," said Thomas, "and that's why he left."

The atmosphere of the village hall was already smoke-filled when they got there. Thomas found it like walking into a wall of warmth, but those sitting near the door begged him to shut it quickly. It was obviously something you got used to. The hall was crowded and there was only room near the front. He found three seats and turned to look about him, but the Rector was already on the platform. He welcomed the audience with the pious wish that they would both enjoy the concert and give generously in a good cause.

"The bank will foreclose if they don't," came audibly from the direction of the doctor, and the concert began with a laugh.

It went on with a laugh, too, though not all of the items were meant to be funny.

The first was a song sung by a lugubrious man with a red nose, from which they progressed to a recitation. Thomas, who had thought never to hear again "The Boy Stood On The Burning Deck" was enchanted. He stole a glance at Tad. He just looked dazed.

Then there came a young man with an electric guitar who went down very well with a certain element at the back of the hall. They raised visible dust by stamping their feet on the floor.

It wasn't the only foot stamping to be done. A harassed woman came on stage and sat down at the piano, struck a chord and said loudly, "One . . . two . . . THREE." On trooped a succession of small children who performed an obscure ritual round a fairy.

This was even more popular, and the curtain for the interval came down to loud applause.

In the cheerful hubbub of conversation which followed

Thomas sought out Mr. Martindale, and brought him over to Tad to introduce him.

The Rector shook hands and lifted one tufted white eyebrow enquiringly. "So you've come back to see how we're getting on, Sir Thaddeus, and like Mr. Harding, to see if justice can be done."

Tad reddened. "I think it's a bit late for justice but I'd certainly like to know the truth."

"One has a way of following the other," said Mr. Martindale, "Mr. Harding here has made some remarkable progress already and some surprising discoveries."

"Precious few deductions though," put in Thomas.

"I think on the whole they come better later anyway," murmured the Rector. "If you will forgive the tautology, a deduction is not like a conclusion, you know, something that can be jumped to. But," warmly, "whatever has brought you, we are glad to see you in Easterbrook."

Tad's features creased into a smile. "Murder most foul brought me," he said. "The family skeleton in the family cupboard."

The second half of the concert went with a swing, too, as far as the majority of the audience were concerned. Only Tad continued to look bemused. He roused himself at one stage to whisper wonderingly to Thomas: "Do they get paid for this?" and on being assured that they did not, sank back into his seat into apparent torpor.

Thomas, too, let his attention wander after a while. His mind slipped back, as it usually did when unoccupied, to the Barbary mystery. Tad's arrival was a help and an unexpected pleasure, but it still left many things unsolved. Suppose Bertram had had a hand in killing his nephew, and suppose that Sir Richard and Giles Shambrook were guilty too, how was he, Thomas Harding, going to prove it a hundred and fifty years later?

His eyes strayed among the audience and came to rest on the Rector. He was sitting in the front row putting up a convincing appearance of being amused by an amateur comedian. He had put his finger on the heart of the Barbary problem. "Find out why the boy was murdered," he had said, "and you will know then who killed him." Thomas stirred on the uncomfortable wooden chair. He was no nearer knowing why Toby had been murdered now than the day he found him.

He roused himself when he heard clapping. That was for the man with the red nose again, who had been singing "The Miller's Song".

Then there came a soprano, and a comedian who wasn't funny and one who was. And a child with a violin whom Thomas would have strangled. Dora leaned over and said sentimentally, "Doesn't he look sweet?"

Thomas growled something indistinguishable.

"You'd never think it was the same boy, would you?" she whispered.

"What same boy?"

"He brings our papers in the mornings."

He was followed by a tall thin man from the grocer's shop who said "The Vicar of Bray" in a monotone, and then the small children came back for the finale. They had lost some of their awe of the stage now, and the harassed woman at the piano had her work cut out to keep both time and order. Clearly neither mattered to the audience, and the final curtain came down to noisy clapping.

Thomas got up to go.

"So you didn't have anyone there after all, did you, Mr. Harding?" said a voice at his elbow, "for all that you thought that you did."

He spun round on his heel, away from Dora and Tad. "Mrs. Fenny!"

Her gaunt features nodded. "That's right, Mr. Harding. My Alan wasn't there after all, was he? When you sent for the police to come and have a look in that old cupboard of yours."

"No. No, he wasn't." Thomas didn't care to have the hide called an old cupboard by anybody. "But he might have been, you can see that."

"He might have been anywhere," she said.

Thomas bent his head towards her. "He's not doing himself any good leading everyone a dance like this. Besides, they're bound to catch him in the end. They always do, you know."

She shook her head triumphantly. "Not now. They won't find Alan there now."

He spoke in a low voice. "I shouldn't talk like that if I were you, Mrs. Fenny. He's not out of the wood yet, you know. And he may be in danger. So may you."

"It won't be for long, Mr. Harding," she said, drawing herself up. She was not without dignity, for all her shabby clothes and prosaic surroundings.

Something in the way she said it made him look up. "You've got news of him, haven't you?" he said in a flash of insight.

"No, Mr. Harding, not exactly. I've always had news of him you see, but—"

"I thought as much . . ."

She gave him one of her odd smiles. "But you might say I'm hoping to have news *for* him soon."

"I don't like the sound of that, Mrs. Fenny."

"No? There's no call for you to worry. He's quite comfortable where he is, but it won't be for long now anyway. And then everything'll be all right again."

Thomas looked about him unhappily. There were several people within earshot, and Mrs. Fenny was not troubling to keep her voice down.

"You mean he's going to give himself up?" he suggested, more optimistically than he felt.

She flashed him her queer smile again and included several bystanders in her reply.

"What? Alan give himself up for a crime he didn't commit? No, Mr. Harding, Alan won't give himself up until the murderer does, but that won't be long now."

Thomas looked round about him but could read nothing from the faces of her audience. They were all of the village. He, Thomas Harding, was the outsider. Their expressions gave nothing away; they were united in their silence. Charlie Ford was there, perspiring gently in the heat of the crowded little hall, and Cousens, the church organist, without his cassock for once, and, at the back of the little group, Gladys, still with her apron on. She had been in the tiny kitchen helping with the refreshments.

"Your son should go straight to the police, Mrs. Fenny," he said sharply. "And so should you if you know anything."

Her harsh voice grated on his ears. "You can't be sure of the police acting."

"Yes, you can," he snapped quickly.

"Ah," she croaked, "but not acting in the way my Alan
would want."

Thomas kept his temper with difficulty. The woman was
acting like a lunatic to imply that she knew who the
murderer was or even where her son was hidden. He
sought for a way to quieten her.

"Your Alan has more sense than to take the law into his
own hands, I'm sure," he said reasonably. "Besides, he
would have to know for certain who killed his wife—and
only the police and a trial by jury could establish that
beyond any doubt."

"Alan knows," she said confidently. "And he's got proof
and it's in a safe place." She gave a brittle laugh. "It's
somewhere where you wouldn't expect to find evidence
for murder." She stared round the circle of listeners.
"You'll all know soon. You'll have proof enough that Alan is
innocent."

"We don't need proof. We all know that," interposed
Charlie Ford, edging his burly form towards her.

She laughed again. "And my Alan's somewhere where
you wouldn't expect to find him either."

"Now then, now then," said Ford. "That's enough of
that, else you'll be worrying Mr. Harding here."

"It's not me who should be worried," retorted Thomas,
"but—"

"No," agreed Ford, cutting him short. "I'll see you
home tonight, Mrs. Fenny. And that'll save us all from
worrying."

He shepherded her away, his bulky form hiding her
from Thomas and preventing him seeing if Mrs. Fenny
went willingly or not.

He turned back to Dora and Tad, his mind completely
distracted by the oddly provocative behaviour of Mrs.
Fenny. Had their entire conversation been staged for the
benefit of somebody else? Was there, then, method in her
apparent madness—had she been trying to get the murderer to show his hand or did she really know who he was
and wanted him to hear of the fact? If she had stood on the
platform and announced to the assembled company that
she knew his name, she could hardly have made it more
public.

And why on earth had she picked on him to talk to about it anyway? His gaffe about sending for the police to look in the hide oughtn't automatically to involve him in Alan Fenny's real whereabouts.

The moon was shining as the trio walked back to the Manor. Thomas was glad enough to get out of the hot and dusty village hall, but he was still uneasy about Mrs. Fenny. Tad was trying to be non-committal to Dora about the concert.

"Very interesting, Mrs. Harding, very interesting indeed."

"What did you think of our soprano?"

"Well, I'm no musician, Mrs. Harding, but I'm sure she would be good if only I knew something about music."

"And the comedian?" mischievously.

"Now which one would that have been?"

Dora laughed aloud. "Tad, I'm not sure myself."

Thomas had meant to talk to Tad about the Barbarys again that night, but Mrs. Fenny's dramatic conversation had made too great an impact on him, and instead he poured out the sad story of the strangled wife and missing husband.

Tad listened in silence—it was one of his nicest points—and then, when Thomas had done, said, "I don't blame the guy for disappearing. No, sir, I'd have done the same myself. Who's going to believe he didn't do it unless he's got proof?"

"But Tad . . ."

"I guess I'd have to go for the chap who did it on my own in case they put me in the hot seat first," said Tad firmly.

"But Tad," protested Dora, "this is England. We don't convict innocent people. He's got nothing to fear if he is innocent."

"Except circumstantial evidence apparently . . ."

Dora shivered. "What has Tad come back to! Not a typical, peaceful English village at all, but murder and suspicion."

Tad took her by the arm and said gravely, "Don't forget, Mrs. Harding, that when Bertram Barbary left Easterbrook it was for those very same reasons."

Thomas nodded, forgetting it was dark. "That's right, Tad. Murder and suspicion—in that order."

"Sure thing, Mr. Harding." Then, with an attempt at lightness, he added, "Perhaps the wheel has come full circle now."

If the village concert had been Tad's introduction to England, Thomas felt that his own introduction to the real Tad came the next morning when they took him to church. They went in very good time for the service.

Tad, who had thought the Manor old, was taken aback by the antiquity of the stout little church.

"Saxon?" he echoed wonderingly.

"In parts," said Thomas. "Not very much."

"But I guess that was before William the Conqueror."

"That's right."

"Domesday?" said Tad, on a rising inflection of excitement. "Do you mean to say this was in the Domesday Book?"

Thomas nodded. "It was. I came across it in one of those county histories I turned up. They mention Easterbrook and the church and Westerbrook, too, if it comes to that."

"Where's that?"

"Nowhere now. It was over the other side of the river, but it's disappeared."

"Sunk without trace?"

"Except in Domesday." Thomas led the way forward. "The nave's Norman and so's the chancel."

Tad stood in the middle of the aisle and looked about him.

A door opened behind them and the first of the regular Sunday morning congregation began to come in for Matins.

"The windows," said Thomas softly, "are Early English."

"It's no good," said Tad. "I'm still trying to assimilate William the Conqueror."

Thomas and Dora led the way ahead of him and stopped near a pew in the front.

"Is this yours?" asked Tad.

"No," retorted Thomas with a solemn smile. "Yours."

Tad knelt down and gazed about him at the memorials to his forebears. A few minutes later he was hissing sibilantly into Thomas's ear.

"I had no idea the Barbarys—well—*mattered* quite so much. Back home in Detroit they didn't count. No, sir, not outside Mike's saloon." He looked ruefully at Thomas. 'And not very much inside either towards the end."

"Most important people in the village from 1587 to 1870," said Thomas promptly. "Then they died out over here. Sir Walter was the last."

He was quite prepared to give a dissertation on the subject there and then—and Tad to listen to him—had not a frown from Dora silenced them both. The organ had suddenly come to life and the Rector was following the choirboys up the nave.

The service wound its way slowly through its ritual phrases and time-honoured responses. The congregation was pleased to be delivered from, among other hazards, battle, murder and sudden death.

Thomas's mind was brought back to the present and Tad jerked out of a state of bemused wonderment by the Rector welcoming from the pulpit the present baronet on his return to Easterbrook. As most of the present inhabitants of the village were sitting behind him they were able to stare uninhibitedly at the back of Tad's neck. Thomas saw a dull red flush creeping up it and sympathetically averted his eyes.

Thomas and Tad stayed behind in the church after the service, leaving Dora to walk home alone.

Thomas led the way to the church tower and pushed back the curtain to show Tad the Barbary benefactions. Tad squinted at the darkened boards.

"The good Sir Richard meant to be remembered, didn't he?"

"Meant to be remembered as good," amended Thomas. "He would have been remembered all right if anyone had seen him kill Toby."

From there they went back to the Barbary family pew at the front of the church and looked up at the memorials to the gallant Colonel Sir Toby and the good Sir Richard.

"I guess I knew not to believe what I read in newspa-

pers," said Tad thoughtfully, "but, you know, until now I
would have taken anything carved in stone as gospel."

"Don't forget," said Thomas, amused, "that all our
suspicions of Sir Richard are pure conjecture. In spite of
all I've said, we haven't a shred of proof, and we haven't
found a single clue to motive."

"We will," said the voice of young America, "if we go at
it."

There was a step behind them. The Rector was walking
up the aisle.

Thomas pointed to the memorial tablet on the wall
above the pew. "Sir Thaddeus isn't going to believe what
he sees writ in stone any more."

The Rector smiled faintly. "Are all chisellers English?"

Tad looked at the clergyman respectfully. "No, sir, I
guess not."

"I've been showing off the church," said Thomas,
shifting the conversational ground quickly. "It's hard to
believe it's quite so old."

"It's very peaceful here, too, sir, isn't it?" said Tad to the
Rector in a lowered voice. "I guess history has passed it by
here in this little village."

"Not quite." The Reverend Cyprian Martindale was not
the man to agree to a platitude. "The Black Death carried
off one of my predecessors and most of his flock, and
Cromwell's men gave it quite a pasting a bit later on. The
South window," he turned and pointed to it. "That's new
glass."

"The Civil War?" hazarded Tad. "You had one of those
too, didn't you?"

"Hitler," said the rector.

"It hasn't," said Tad wryly, "missed out on anything yet
has it? Not ever murder."

The Rector nodded. "One thing has struck me very
much about your murder and all that you have told me
about this Richard Barbary. There is no record of anyone
liking the man. Now, popularity is no great guide to
worth, but the truly generous are rarely not liked at all."

"You think, sir, that Easterbrook knew about the murder?" asked Tad.

"I think that when no body was found in the mill dam

they guessed that evil was afoot. Mind you, they would
say nothing—as they have said nothing about Alan
Fenny—but I think they would know. And all the benefactions in the world wouldn't impress them then."

Thomas nodded in agreement. "The motive's our
stumbling block."

"You could say that motive was always the most important thing, you know." The veins standing out on the
clergyman's hands served to remind Thomas that he was
talking to an old man.

"Do they," he asked delicately, "know why Mary Fenny
died?"

Mr. Martindale rested his hands on the back of a pew.
"That is not for me to conjecture. All I can say is that she
was not an heiress, nor greedy. Nor did she stand in
anyone's way."

"Then . . ."

"You see, I knew Mary Fenny, and knew her for what
she was—a very good-looking girl indeed, but not a
strongminded one."

"Not the sort of person to go to the police about
anything?"

"Married to an idealist, too," went on the Rector without hearing. "Not clever enough, perhaps, to know danger
for what it was when she saw it . . ." He began to move
away. "Perhaps you are right, Mr. Harding, to take refuge
in the past after all."

"Phew!" said Tad, when the Rector had gone into the
vestry, "you people sure specialise in double meanings.
Where do we go from here?"

"Home for lunch. I'll show you the Barbary almshouses
on the way."

He led Tad across the village green towards the river.

"There they are," he said, pointing. "The Barbary
Charities."

Tad followed his gaze and then said uncertainly,
"They're kind of cute, aren't they? You know—tricked up."

"They are the genuine article all right. They're not even
tricked up with hot water. But I know what you mean.
Picture postcard."

"And the good Sir Richard built them?"

"In 1816 for the poor and needy of the parish."

"His servants," supplemented Tad drily. "A real philanthropist this Sir Richard. Tell me," he waved his hand to embrace the village, "did he do anything else that looked good and wasn't?"

"That's a good question."

"In the circumstances . . ."

"He built a new bridge across the river," said Thomas slowly, "and that meant a stretch of new road from the Manor to the village. I've been wondering why he did that."

"He'll have had his reasons," drawled Tad. "You can bet your life on that."

But Thomas was pursuing his own line of thought.

"It was a really old road, much earlier than Sir Richard. It probably connected with a ford over the river long before the days of bridges."

Tad sighed audibly. "That's what I can't get used to over here. Everything has been going on for so long."

Fourteen

MONDAY was a fine crisp morning and Thomas got up for breakfast for the first time since the ill-fated visit of Archibald Mellon. He went through his post between the toast and marmalade, opening the large envelope first.

The missive inside had come from the said Archibald Mellon. He smoothed out the sheets and began to read.

"My dear Harding,

In spite of the inconvenience of not being able to see you again as arranged I have pursued the matter of the priest's hole in your house. There was undoubtedly a good deal of recusancy in this part of the world throughout Tudor times, though it diminished in direct proportion to the measures taken to suppress it.

I find that the Cloakes of Easterbrook were a noted Catholic family and definitely gave shelter to Jesuit priests both passing through and for longer periods. As you know these priests were mostly trained abroad, and the position of Easterbrook within easy reach of the coast makes me even more sure that the Manor was used frequently by them.

At one time the Cloakes almost certainly maintained a resident priest because it was recorded that it was for the harbouring of a Jesuit that Gerald Cloake was imprisoned. That means that there will have been a chapel somewhere, or, at the very least, a room in which Mass was customarily celebrated.

Nicholas Owen, about whom we spoke, was the master builder of refuges such as yours, and I have been able to confirm that he was known to have been

in Calleshire at one stage in his career. I think we may
assume that he built your hide. A further pointer
would be the discovery of either a bolt hole within the
hide or another exit from it."

Thomas read the letter carefully and then passed it over
to Tad.

"Nothing to help us with the Barbary problem," he
said, "but interesting all the same. One of these days,
when I've got time..." he stopped, and looked across at
his wife, smiling. "Do you realise that's the first time I've
used that expression since we moved here?"

She filled his cup. "I used to get very tired of hearing
it."

"You did?"

"In London."

"Oh, I hadn't thought of that."

"On the odd occasions when I saw you in passing," said
his wife, "before you left for the office or when you came
home. Unless you were too tired to speak." She swept up
Tad's cup. "More coffee for you, Tad?"

"Thank you," Tad grinned. "What is it you are going to
do when you've got time, Mr. Harding?"

"Read up about the Cloake family and what Mellon calls
'recusancy'."

"Before our time, these Cloakes, aren't they?" said Tad,
skimming Mellon's letter.

"Couple of hundred years, I expect," said Thomas.

"Here when the Barbarys landed, you might say?" He
put the letter down. "I guess that makes us a pretty
jumped up lot, don't you?"

Thomas reached for the letter and folded it back into its
envelope. "Not really. The first Sir Tobias bought the
house from Gerald Cloake when he was down on his luck."

"At his own price, I'll bet," said the young realtor.

"The real estate business hasn't changed much," said
Thomas apologetically. "And Sir Tobias was a business
man, don't forget, a successful merchant adventurer from
the City of London."

"They do make mistakes," said Dora suddenly.

"Who do?"

"Estate agents."

"Not many," said Thomas warmly.

"They should have added 'historical associations' to the advertisement for this house."

"That's true. 'Select your own mystery' you might say."

"As it happens, Mr. Harding," said Tad, "this guy Fenny interests me as much as anything. What do you reckon he's up to?"

Thomas stowed Mellon's letter away in his pocket. Tad was of his own generation all right, a man of the present. "Hiding," he said.

Dora picked up the coffee pot. "I think he's come back for more than shelter. If he'd just wanted to hide he wouldn't have come here where everyone knows him and where the police would expect to find him."

"But his friends . . ."

"A man who strangles his wife doesn't have friends," pronounced Dora firmly. "Only people who used to know him once."

"I guess you've got something there," said Tad. "So he comes back to Easterbrook to find the real murderer, would you say?"

"Not 'find' exactly," qualified Thomas. "I think he may well know—or at least may have guessed—his identity. I reckon he came back to get absolute proof."

Dora shuddered. "Or to provoke the murderer into showing his hand."

"Something like that," said Thomas.

"Your police have searched the village, haven't they?"

"Several times," said Thomas ruefully. "But whoever has got him hidden has him hidden well. There's been neither sight nor sound of him for days. He'll have his reasons."

"Revenge," said Tad succinctly. "The hope of the sweet taste of revenge. What was his wife like?"

"Very good looking according to the Calleford *Courier* photograph—which might have been touched up. Beautiful, according to the Rector, who ought to be an impartial, if not reliable judge."

"Ah," said Tad ambiguously.

"Her parents have a little shop in the High Street—I'll show it to you some time. Middling prosperous, you know.

The police have been there often enough but they can't or won't help."

"Can't, I think," said Dora. "Her mother is quite broken up by all this, and the father is running the business and coping with his wife. Gladys says they don't seem to care one way or another about Alan since Mary died."

"Not the same stuff as Mrs. Fenny, senior, is made of," commented Tad.

"I don't think they come like her often," said Thomas. "I was quite glad to see her safe and sound in church yesterday after all that talk on Saturday night in the village hall."

Dora stood up. "I don't want to hurry you two but it is Monday morning and Gladys and I are going to be busy this morning."

Tad glanced at her uneasily. "I guess it's about time I looked in at The George, Mrs. Harding, I'm making a lot of extra work here."

"Indeed, you are not, Tad," retorted Dora roundly. "It's just that I don't want either of you underfoot while I'm working. You can both stay in the drawing-room while we get on."

But the prospect of being imprisoned in the drawing-room with the energetic Tad did not appeal to Thomas and it was not long before he suggested a visit to Calleford.

"Tad can drive," he said, "and I can show him those old Calleford *Couriers*. I think he ought to see them for himself. I feel fine now and I won't walk far."

So Tad steered Thomas's car cautiously along the left-hand side of the road through Easterbrook and out on the Calleford road.

They parked near the Minster.

"A big church?" asked Tad.

"Cathedral. Small as cathedrals go but cathedral all the same."

Tad pointed to the green carpet of grass that surrounded it. "Does this come with all your old buildings?"

"Supplied with every order," said Thomas gravely, steering him down the road past the public library.

"A local girl who made good?" said Tad, pointing to the Crown" half of the pair of statues.

Thomas screwed up his eyes. "I think that's 'literature'."

"Who's her friend?"

"Art."

"You don't say."

"They are also known as the Rose and Crown."

"Something to do with the Wars of the Roses?" drawled
ad.

"Only remotely," said Thomas.

They turned into the offices of the Calleford *Courier.*
he clerk remembered Thomas and led him and Tad
raight down to the basement. Tad gazed round the
ook-lined walls, visibly impressed.

"Gee, I guess the history of this whole town is bound up
here."

The elderly clerk adjusted his pince-nez. "Dear me, no.
ardly any of it really. *The Courier* only goes back to
789. Next to no time at all where Calleford is concerned."

"No?"

"They found remains of Beaker people not far from
ere, you know, and the Romans had a camp here. Quite a
g one because it was one of the places where you could
rd the Calle river."

"Gee," said Tad again.

"And the Minster," added the clerk gravely, "is by no
eans new."

Thomas soon found the volume dated 1815. Tad set it on
e table for him.

"Guess this is what they call heavy reading, Mr.
arding. Now, whereabouts is this report?"

"The first Friday in May on the front page."

Tad leafed carefully through the yellowed pages. They
d not turn easily and he needed both hands to smooth
em into place. And then he fell still, his head bent
tently over a page. Thomas found himself a seat and
atched in silence as the fifteenth baronet of Easterbrook
ad of the disappearance of the only son of the eighth of
s line.

It was very quiet in *The Courier* basement. Thomas
ticed that a spider had spun herself a web from the

bottom of the bound leather volume for the year 1887 to the top of that on the shelf below, dated 1923. How long was it, he mused, since anyone had wanted to look up anything in those years?

Tad lifted his head from his reading.

"It's the phoniest story I've ever read."

"It doesn't quite hold water," agreed Thomas mildly. "I thought you would like to see the original."

"The original I'd like to see would be Toby's precious Uncle Richard," muttered Tad fiercely.

"Alas," said Thomas. "Everything except his memory is beyond revenge."

"As for his memory . . ."

"Yes?"

Tad tapped the yellowed paper. "There must be some way of . . . of . . . unhallowing it."

"I doubt it."

"But—"

"We can't prove anything," said Thomas, "but even if we could . . ."

"Well?"

"No one would be interested."

"But . . ."

"It wouldn't be the first time the public memory has been misled," said Thomas. "Nor the last."

Tad subsided, muttering.

"Turn up the boy's father's death," advised Thomas. "That rings true. I'm about to disturb a spider."

He moved away from Tad and pulled out the Calleford Courier for 1923; the spider would have to select some other volume now on which to pin her trap. He didn't find it a dull year. As much had happened in 1923 as in any other. He turned over the pages, one by one, only half aware of Tad doing the same thing across the room.

He heard a grunt of satisfaction at one stage and assumed that Tad had found "the lamentable intelligence from the field of Waterloo". Then more rustlings of pages and the silence of concentration.

For himself Thomas found the advertisements of 1923 as interesting as anything else, and as much a mirror of contemporary life as the actual news stories.

"Mr. Harding." Tad was speaking to him in a low excited voice. "Come right over here and take a look at this will you?"

Thomas looked up. "Found something?"

"I think so."

Thomas went across and peered over his shoulder. "Did I miss something important?"

"Not really. This was before the murder. I was just turning back to sort of put myself in the picture with the times, if you know what I mean."

Thomas nodded. "And what did you find?"

"This!" Tad laid a finger on the newsprint.

It was quite a short report.

Mr. Richard Barbary, younger brother of Sir Toby Barbary of Easterbrook, had failed to meet his debts at his London gaming club.

"I take it," said Tad simply, "that this means something."

"Several things," said Thomas slowly. "The end of his fun and games unless he could find the money quickly."

"He couldn't, could he?"

"How do we know?"

Tad tapped the paper. "This report wouldn't have got as far as Calleford, would it, if the money had been forthcoming?"

"That's true. That means . . ."

"That brother Sir Toby wasn't coming to the rescue," said Tad.

"He probably did to begin with," said Thomas.

"But not this time," said Tad. "Else they wouldn't have gone ahead with a report like this."

"Warning everyone," added Thomas, "that Richard Barbary was no good and Sir Toby wasn't going to help any more."

"Not even for the good of the family name?"

"There comes a point," said Thomas wisely, "when it's no good going on preserving it from the inveterate bad hat."

Tad swivelled round on his chair and looked at Thomas. "Do you realise, Mr. Harding, that this is the first time we have found anything—anything at all—that goes to show that the good Sir Richard wasn't a pure, upright, all-American boy?"

Thomas grinned. "He sounds an out-and-out rake to me."

"And then some . . . What does all this mean murder-wise?"

"Motive," said Thomas definitely.

"I don't quite see . . ."

"Let me explain the quaint old English custom of primogeniture."

"You mean," said Tad, when he had done, "that Richard murdered young Toby so he would inherit?"

"That's my guess now. It was the only conceivable way he would ever come in to any money. It's no good him killing his brother because the property goes to the boy willy-nilly."

"So he kills the boy and he's bound to come into the money himself."

"Sooner or later. When his brother dies. I dare say he could borrow on his expectations until then. Of course, he may have planned to kill him too. We don't know."

"More difficult."

"More suspicious, too. We may be wrong, of course, in all our suppositions, but we've got Richard on his beam ends . . . when?"

"End of March, 1815."

"London too hot to hold him and his brother not prepared to give him the money. And in early May, the boy dies."

"Stage One," said Tad Barbary, "of Plan A, if you ask me."

Thomas had introduced Tad to the un-American activity of a glass of sherry before luncheon. They foregathered in the drawing-room and raised their glasses to the panelling.

"It's funny to think that if that boy hadn't been killed and put in there all those years ago I wouldn't be here today."

"You wouldn't have been Sir Thaddeus either," Dora reminded him.

Tad flushed and then said lightly, "I don't think that would have been any great loss to the world."

"Too soon to say," said Thomas gravely.

Tad smiled. "I reckon there's a place in every American home for a priest's hole like yours. You'd be quite safe if anyone called and it's too small for television."

"I still don't like to think of it as a vault," said Dora.

Tad set his glass down, the sherry barely tasted. "Poor little Toby. There can't have been many stranger burial places. It must have been quite a performance getting the body in there."

The older man looked up. "Three strong men could have done it."

"Sir Richard, Bertram, and who else?"

"Giles Shambrook."

"I was forgetting him."

"Sir Richard didn't," said Thomas drily.

"One of the things I can't understand," went on Tad with disarming diffidence, "is how they managed to murder a fifteen-year-old boy without someone seeing them, hide his body and then bring it here. Unless, of course, they killed him here too."

"I don't think they did that," said Thomas. "His mother was living here in the house—was mistress of it at the time. That would be tempting fate too much."

"Well then . . ."

"Darkness covered a great deal in those days. There were no street lights and people didn't go out much after dark. I think he was in this priest's hole not long after his father died, probably soon after his mother left. Sir Richard could have wedged the panel perhaps, or put a great big piece of furniture in front of it so that the servants wouldn't open it. They were sent off to the new almshouses early the next year so that they wouldn't put two and two together when they saw the panelling."

"How horribly efficient you make it seem," Dora said quietly. "Everything so well planned—it makes it twice as cold-blooded."

Thomas smiled. He could never understand why women hated to be thought efficient. It was not a virtue with them. Even Miss Porteous, the admirable Miss Porteous, had preferred other compliments.

"Of course we don't know for certain that Bertram was involved," said Thomas, "but—"

"I think he was," said Tad. "I don't think he *planned* t
come over to the States in 1815. It wouldn't have been
good year for British immigrants." Tad, too, could be ver
dry. "Washington would still be smouldering, and a cha
called Andrew Jackson had just beaten off an attack b
you—er—by us—by . . ."

"By the British."

"By the British at New Orleans."

"So we can assume that Bertram was in it all right."

"I'm afraid so," said the youngest sprig of Bertram'
line. "Up to the neck, I expect."

"So," said Thomas judicially, "we can assume they fake
the accident and daren't let the body be found because i
proved murder."

"That's right," agreed Tad. "It was probably too difficul
to fake an accident and let everyone have a good look a
the body."

"And that way," said Thomas thoughtfully, "if anythin
did go wrong, nothing could be laid at Sir Richard's doo
anyway."

"Except suspicion."

"I doubt if that was going to worry him. Certainly nc
after Waterloo."

"That was a bonus for him."

"But if it hadn't happened," said Tad, "I wouldn't hav
been unbearably surprised to hear that Sir Toby had had
fatal fall from his horse."

"Or fallen down a flight of steps," said Thomas.

"Or sickened of the palsy," contributed Dora. "Or ha
they stopped dying of that by then?"

"So," said Tad presently, "they killed young Toby, whicl
meant they had a body on their hands. Can we work ou
what they did then?"

"They hid it somewhere," said Thomas. "They found hi
fishing rod and tangled it in some trees by the river wher
it was sure to be found—oh, and they threw one of hi
shoes in the water, too."

"Clever, that. To only throw one, I mean. Two woul
have been overdoing it. Leaves a nice mental picture c
the lad struggling to kick the other one off."

Thomas smiled faintly. "The psychological approach at work."

"What happened to the other shoe? It wasn't still on the body?"

"No."

"And that wouldn't have rotted as quickly as the fabric," mused Tad. "Then what, do you suppose?"

"After the faking of the accident, you mean? Presumably after a while they started searching for him and that evening his Uncle Richard 'found' the fishing rod. History doesn't record who fished the shoe out, but Richard and Bertram would have taken good care it wasn't either of them. Then Giles Shambrook comes up with this story about having seen Toby fishing from the river bank at about three o'clock in the afternoon."

"Watertight."

"A corpse who had died from drowning would have been—er—conclusive."

"Point taken," said Tad. "So what these guys needed more than anything was somewhere to park that body while they did a bit of lying low and keeping quiet."

"A very safe place. And then Napoleon saw to their chief worry—that boy's father."

"Plan A, Stage Two."

"After that," said Thomas obliquely, "it would be plain sailing."

"So they took the body from point X to this priest's hole, thought up a scheme for getting the servants away, plastered up the wall, destroyed the written reference to it and lived happily ever after."

"Sir Richard may have done," said Thomas. "It doesn't sound as if Bertram did, and we don't know about Giles Shambrook."

"Come to think of it," said Tad, "we don't know much about either of them."

Thomas waved a hand towards a pile of notes. "Help yourself."

At four o'clock Thomas came downstairs from his afternoon rest. Tad was sitting in a corner, surrounded by notebooks.

Dora was pushing a tea trolley into the drawing-room. Tad sprang to his feet to help her in with it.

"Tea at four is one of the nicest things about England," he said.

"And manners are the best part of a matriarchy," observed Thomas, coming in behind his wife. "Any luck with your researches, Tad? You look like the cat that swallowed the canary."

"Do I?" He grinned. "Pity. I was trying to practise some typical English self-control."

"I shouldn't bother," said Thomas briefly. "What have you found?"

"The reason why no one saw the crime."

"You have? Well done!"

"The Easterbrook Fair was held on May 1st." He wrinkled his brow and looked very American. "Don't you people still celebrate May Day?"

"Only some of us."

"But how clever of you, Tad," said Dora, placidly pouring out tea. "How did you discover that?"

"The history of the village that Mr. Harding copied out says that there is a fair yearly on May Day and that day—May 1st—is the date that the Calleford *Courier* gives for Toby's death."

"Of course!" explained Thomas. "Everyone would be at the fair except our three villains."

"And Toby Barbary." His face changed suddenly. "I say, I've just thought of something. There was a war on. Perhaps they didn't have fairs in wartime."

Thomas shook his head. "They would have had them. It wasn't total war in those days. Just military war."

"You still had your bread and circuses?"

Thomas stirred his tea without listening. "It was premeditated murder then. They chose that day on purpose when the attention of every man, woman and child was elsewhere."

Tad pulled a wry face. "And I thought I'd squeezed those notes dry."

"I don't know that we can get any further," said Thomas. "Not now. Unless . . ."

"Yes?"

"We could walk as far as the churchyard after tea and
e if Giles Shambrook lived to a ripe old age."

But they could not find any tombstone with that name
n it. They quartered the churchyard and there was no
rave of any Giles Shambrook of Yew Tree Cottage.

If the Rector had not happened to come out of the
hurch after saying the office of Evensong they never
ould have found it.

Mr. Martindale listened to the tale of their search.

"Of course," said Thomas, "Shambrook may have taken
ight like Bertram Barbary and gone, but he had quite a
ake here in Easterbrook in that cottage and his work,
o, whatever that might have been."

"There's one place you won't have seen," said the
ector, leading them to the far corner of the churchyard
nd pushing open a small iron gate set in the wall. "It's
orth a look in here."

There were several mounds in the grass in the small
nclosure but few headstones. There was one though that
ore initials that could conceivably have been G.H.S. and
e date, which was clearer, was 1825.

"It came after the barbarous burials at cross-roads with a
take through the heart," said Mr. Martindale. "And a
ood thing too."

"Yes?" said Thomas, not understanding him.

"Unconsecrated ground," said the cleric, "to be used for
ny that die unbaptised, or excommunicate, or that have
id violent hands upon themselves."

Fifteen

THEY got back to the Manor just as Dora put the last of t
supper dishes on the dining-room table.

"Well," she said, when they were all three seated. "D
you find him?"

"He's busy just now. He's coming along here as soon
he can."

"A ghost," said Dora. "That will be nice."

Thomas looked blankly across the table at his wife.

"You left," she reminded him, "to look for the grave
the churchyard of a man called Giles Shambrook."

"I was thinking about Charlie Ford," confessed Thoma
"We happened to see him down by the church wi
Gladys and Mrs. Fenny, and I asked him to come up
see me. There's still a little matter of some wiring tha
want to have out with him."

"Did you find Giles Shambrook?" asked his wife.

"We think so."

"But we can't be sure," chimed in Tad.

"Whose side was he on?"

"I guess this business isn't like a baseball game, M
Harding," said Tad. "It sure is difficult to see who is
whose side."

"It certainly isn't cricket," said Dora tartly; a rema
which delighted Tad, who declared it was one of the thin
he had come to England to hear.

"I thought you'd come to avenge the memory of yo
ancestors," said Thomas mildly.

"I don't think it's going to work out that way," said T:
ruefully, "do you?"

"Since you ask me, no. Especially considering where v
found Giles Shambrook."

"I have been trying," said Dora patiently, "to get one or other of you to tell me where that was for the last ten minutes."

"Unconsecrated ground," said Thomas.

Dora raised an eyebrow. "Suicide?"

"Could be." He looked round. "Salt anybody? We only get there by exclusion, of course. He's unlikely to have died unbaptised, is he? I mean every infant was done in those days, wasn't it?"

Dora nodded. "Besides Mr. Martindale would look that up for you in the Parish Registers."

"I'll make a note of that. And as for dying excommunicate, I don't think that would have happened either without there being some note of it somewhere."

"It wouldn't have been an everyday occurrence," said Dora. "Not in Easterbrook."

"You're getting quite parochial, my dear."

"I guess," drawled Tad, "that he's just as unlikely to have committed suicide if it comes to that."

"Why?" asked Dora.

"Because that would have been just too many strokes of luck for Sir Richard, that's why."

"You've got a good point there."

"When did Sir Richard give Shambrook the freehold of that cottage, Mrs. Harding?"

In a flash Thomas had left the table and was thumbing through the Barbary notebooks.

"The doctor," murmured Dora, "said something about simple, peaceful meals, eaten quietly. I can't remember his exact wording but I don't suppose—"

"1820," said Thomas unabashed. "I saw the copy of the actual instrument. My solicitors sent it with the deeds of the Manor."

Tad nodded. "He wasn't too greedy too soon."

"No." Thomas came back and sat down. "He would know, I think, when he was on to a good thing."

"Wait until the hoo-ha died down and then speak."

"That's right. He could be sure that Sir Richard wouldn't leave Easterbrook. All he had to do was wait until he felt really secure as lord of the manor and then come and ask him for payment for services rendered."

"Or silence."

"Comes to the same thing, doesn't it? It looks as if h[e] got the cottage five years after the murder but I dare sa[y] he had one or two small contributions in between."

"It's quite significant, isn't it," put in Dora, "that Si[r] Richard gave him property."

"I don't see that it is," said Thomas.

"This man Shambrook must have felt pretty confident t[o] get an actual building out of Sir Richard. He wouldn't hav[e] wanted to part with anything so... tangible. I mean people would know, wouldn't they?"

"I get you, Mrs. Harding," said Tad. "You think thi[s] character Shambrook wasn't above letting Easterbroo[k] know he was in a position to twist Sir Richard's arm?"

"Something like that," said Dora. "Sort of showing off [a] bit."

"I shouldn't have wanted to play that sort of game wit[h] Sir Richard Barbary," said Thomas.

"Nor me," said Tad decisively. "And look where it go[t] him anyway."

"A suicide's grave." Dora shivered.

"He didn't commit suicide," retorted Tad. "You don'[t] commit suicide if you've been given a nice little house fo[r] you and your heirs in perpetuity, and probably have a[n] equally nice little annuity coming in too."

"With built-in safeguards against inflation," said Thoma[s] the business man.

Dora sighed. "I don't suppose you do. Giles Shambroo[k] must have wanted a little more than Sir Richard wa[s] prepared to give."

"Can we find out how he died?" asked Tad.

Thomas shook his head. "I doubt it, but we can alway[s] try the Parish Registers. However it was though, it mus[t] have *looked* sufficiently like suicide to persuade the recto[r] of the day to insist on unconsecrated ground."

"You probably need two to fake an accident," said Tad sardonically.

"Three's better," said Thomas, grinning.

"I know, I know. I haven't forgotten the—what is i[t] called? The blot on the family escutcheon. Bertram the Blot—sounds just about right to me."

"No risk of your suffering from ancestor worship," said
Thomas, "is there?"

"How long did Richard live after Shambrook died?"
Dora wanted to know.

Thomas didn't need his notebooks for that. "Ten years.
Until 1835."

"What would have happened to Yew Tree Cottage when
Shambrook died? Would Sir Richard have got it back?"

"Oh, no. That Deed of Gift we saw was quite irrevoca-
ble. The building would have gone to Giles Shambrook's
heirs. I don't think Shambrook would have agreed to any
situation where Sir Richard benefited too directly from his
death."

"He'd have had to keep his wits about him as it was,"
said Tad, "wouldn't he?"

"I'd have kept a weather eye open in his place," admitted Thomas.

Dora sat back. "This Sir Richard doesn't improve on
acquaintance, does he?"

"I think," said Thomas sagaciously, "that Giles
Shambrook got Yew Tree Cottage as a reward for his hand
in the murder of Toby Barbary. Sir Richard doubtless
intended it as a final payment, but Giles Shambrook
probably treated it as something on account and asked for
more."

"And Sir Richard kept him stringing along until the
opportunity for 'suicide' presented itself," finished Tad.

"It's a good job that ancestor of yours did emigrate, Tad.
I don't think he'd have lived to tell the tale if he hadn't."
Thomas pushed his chair back. "A very nice supper, dear,
thank you."

"I should take that as a compliment," said Dora, "if I
thought for one moment that you would remember what
we had for the first course."

"Meat," said Thomas promptly.

"Tad?" Dora asked.

"I guess I'd have said meat too," said Tad uneasily.

Thomas looked up less confidently. "It *was* meat, wasn't
it?"

Dora went out into the kitchen. "A diet of Barbary is all
you want. What you had was best English lamb." The door

shut behind her. It opened a minute later and she can
back.

"I've just thought of something. That ma
Shambrook..."

"Now who's wrapped up in the Barbarys?"

Dora smiled. "They do grow on one, don't they?"

"What was it you thought of, Mrs. Harding?" put i
Tad. "Something important?"

"I don't suppose so," she said briskly, "but it occurred
me that if this man Shambrook was just an ordina
working man in the village as we have always suppose
him to be, then his threats to expose Sir Richard wouldn
carry much weight, would they?"

"Unless he had proof," said Thomas slowly.

Tad pointed in the direction of the drawing-room. "H
could tell them the body was behind the panelling."

"Ah, yes, of course he could, but no one in the village
going to break up the Squire's drawing-room just becaus
a common or garden labourer tells them to."

"That's true," said Thomas, "and there were no polic
to go to with a tale, true or otherwise."

"I see what you mean, Mrs. Harding," said Tad intentl
"Giles Shambrook wouldn't just say to Sir Richard, 'Loo
here, I'll tell everyone you've got a body in the house.' S
Richard would probably laugh and tell him to go righ
ahead, knowing full well he is the most important man i
the place—for miles around perhaps."

"It's a nice idea," said Thomas, "that Giles Shambroo
might have had other evidence besides the body."

"It's a sound one," retorted Tad. "And I'll bet that othe
evidence is why Giles Shambrook had to die. Being wi
ness to a murder ten years before and knowing where th
body was wouldn't count for much if it's the little gu
versus the big guy..."

"There's another thing," said Thomas. "If justice eve
caught up with Sir Richard it would have netted Gile
Shambrook too."

"That's a point," conceded Tad. "This Giles Shambroo
must have known something else, something that woul
convince other people that their squire was a...a..
villain."

The Hardings exchanged smiles at his vehemence.

"Villain is the right word, Tad," said Dora, in case he hould mind. "A good old-fashioned one, too."

"I wonder what he had," mused Thomas.

"I wonder if it's still about," said Tad.

Thomas laughed. "It wasn't yesterday, you know."

"Still," said Tad, "we know quite a bit, don't we? We now how the three of them killed young Toby, and when, nd how they faked the accident, and more-or-less what ecame of the three of them afterwards."

"More or less," agreed Thomas. "We are reasonably ıre that Giles Shambrook was an accomplice to the xtent of bearing false witness and being rewarded with a ouse."

"And his own death warrant."

"And we know that Bertram left the country the year of ıe murder."

"He played chicken pretty quickly," said his great, reat, great, great-grandson.

"Taking with him," continued Thomas, "a legacy of guilt ıat has been handed down to you. And we now think that ;iles Shambrook had some concrete evidence."

"Which, incidentally, wouldn't incriminate himself too ıuch . . ."

". . . That he could hold over Sir Richard's head."

"Which was his undoing."

hey had their coffee in the drawing-room, Dora and 'homas sitting in their accustomed places on either side of ıe fire. Tad took his chair and stood it firmly and squarely ı front of the fire and still shivered slightly at normal ‚nglish room temperature.

"At least that priest wouldn't have been cold in his ide."

"He'd have been very comfortable," said Thomas in a roprietorial sort of way. "Good fresh air, the warmth of ıe chimney, drainage of a sort. All he needed was food nd drink."

Tad grinned. "A bit hair-raising all the same, having ıose what-do-you-call-'ems poking about."

"Pursuivants."

"Having them looking for you."

"Nerve-racking," agreed Thomas, "but don't forget good old Nicholas Owen."

"How come?"

"He'd thought of that, remember?"

Tad shook his head.

"I thought you didn't read that letter very carefully," said Thomas. "The one from Mellon this morning."

"What had Owen thought of?" asked Dora.

"The pursuivants finding the hide. At least so Mellon says in his letter. Owen usually provided a bolt hole within the hide to trick the pursuivants into thinking they'd found an empty hide."

"Have—er—we got one of those?" asked Tad.

Thomas laughed. "I shouldn't think so."

"There's no harm in looking," said Tad.

"If we had had one," said Thomas, "Sir Richard would have put the body in the bolt hole and saved himself the bother of plastering up the hide."

"Only if he'd known about it," pointed out Dora.

"I suppose it could have been there all the time without any of the Barbarys knowing about it," said Thomas doubtfully, "but I should have thought . . ."

"That book," said Dora suddenly.

"What about it?"

"The one that Sir Toby—the boy's father—wrote: he didn't mention it, did he?"

"No," said Thomas unwillingly. "Now you come to mention it, I don't think he did."

"It's worth a look," said Tad.

"Go ahead," said Thomas. "I did start measuring up the whole house but Constable Wilkins took all my calculations away with him."

"There's another thing," said Dora, warming to her theme. "Mr. Mellon kept on saying that this man Owen specialised in secrecy. The Barbarys could have known about the hide all along but not the bolt hole. Perhaps only Gerald Cloake knew about that."

"Perhaps," agreed Thomas indulgently, "but it's pure speculation."

Tad pushed back the panel and stepped inside. "It won't be in the outside wall anyway. That's solid enough."

"Nor against the chimney either," called through
omas. "Mellon went up there."

"Too obvious anyway," said Tad, reappearing at the
trance with a torch. "The floor seems quite firm but it
y not be."

"We haven't any cellars," began Dora, when Tad gave an
cited squeak.

"Say, Mr. Harding, I think I'm on to something. There's
bit of a gap in the flooring." His voice was muffled but
ent. "Could you come?"

Thomas rose and went over to the panelling.

"It's the torch," said Tad. "I need both hands. Could
u just shine it over here from where you're standing
ile I get a grip on this."

Thomas directed the beam towards Tad, who was brac-
g himself to lift one of the large old floorboards.

"Just there—that's right. I think this is loose." He drew
his breath and heaved. "Here it comes."

It lifted slowly in his hands. Thomas shone the torch in
gap the floorboard left in the floor.

Lying full length under the board was Alan Fenny.

Sixteen

THE man blinked in the sudden light and then brought h
hand round to shield his eyes.

"It's Mr. Harding, isn't it?" he said uncertainly.

"God bless my soul," said Thomas.

"I've only seen you the once, Mr. Harding..."

"That day in the church..."

"That's right. I didn't know who you were then but
thought you might be from the Manor. I know most
everybody else in the village. 'Course, I got to know yo
voice quite well after that."

Tad was standing impatiently above him, the heav
board poised on end, half ready to drop it back. "This th
guy everyone's been looking for?"

"Alan Fenny," agreed Thomas.

It was quite a tight fit for a man to lie between th
joists. Once there he would not be able to move. Perha
therein had lain his safety.

"Alan Fenny," said Thomas again, "though he hadn't g
that beard when I saw him last."

Fenny raised himself on one elbow and fingered h
chin. "No razor."

"Have you been in here all the time?"

Fenny looked confused. "I'm sorry, Mr. Harding."

"You came here that day straight from the church."

"That's right."

"Up the old road..."

"It was the best way..."

"I'll bet it was."

Tad shifted the board to a slightly less threateni
angle. "But you haven't been in that...coffin all th
time..."

162

Fenny shook his head. "No, thank God. I just got in here when I heard someone coming to the panel in the wall. There's just time if you're on the alert."

"Like the priests," said Thomas.

Fenny looked blank. "I don't know anything about them. It's a tight enough fit for me under the board—I didn't fancy going in there too often."

"You didn't have to, though, did you?" said Thomas. "When the Inspector came . . ."

"That's right." He grimaced. "You can tell them by their boots. They didn't worry me, Mr. Harding. It was someone else."

"Someone else?"

Fenny nodded. "That's right. Gave me ever such a fright, they did, whoever they were."

Thomas looked mystified. "What sort of a person?"

Fenny shivered. "I don't know but they very nearly found me. Light on their feet, I'll say that for them. All over the place, tapping and calling out. Sort of a high voice."

Thomas's face cleared. "Mellon!"

"I don't know who it was," repeated the young man, "but I thought he'd found me and then he went off up the chimney or something."

"You'd better sit up properly, hadn't you," said Thomas. "You must be cramped like that."

Fenny straightened himself out slowly and stiffly.

"I wasn't," said Thomas, "all that far off the mark then. It made sense to me, the way everything went, and then when the police opened up the hide you weren't there."

Fenny shook himself apologetically. "I was."

Now he was out of the little hole the dominant impression of the man was dust. His hair, his clothes, his hands and face were all covered in a dark dust.

Tad's eyes never left him. "What do you want doing with him, Mr. Harding?"

"I'm blessed if I know, Tad. Send for the police, I suppose."

"Don't do that, Mr. Harding," burst out Fenny. "Not just yet . . . please . . ."

"And why not?"

"There's reasons, Mr. Harding. Not tonight. Please Tomorrow if you like. I won't run away."

"What's happening tonight?"

Fenny shook himself again. "Nothing, Mr. Harding."

"Well then..."

"No, don't send for the police. They wouldn't understand..." He was beseeching now.

There was a snort from Tad at this, but it was Dora t whom Thomas turned with an enquiring look.

"I think, dear," she said, "we ought to ask him if he" hungry."

Fenny dropped his hands helplessly to his sides. "That' very kind of you, Mrs. Harding. No, I'm not hungry."

"But you've been in there for days."

He hung his head without saying anything.

"I fancy," said Thomas mildly, "that Fenny has—er— friends."

"That I have," said the young man earnestly. "Goo friends. Friends that don't believe as how I would hav laid a finger on Mary and are willing to put themselves ou to prove it."

"Sammy!" exclaimed Thomas suddenly. "Fenny, tell m this—do these good friends of yours feed you at nigh time?"

"Yes, Mr. Harding." He looked a bit abashed, and adde hurriedly, "Not but we've been ever so careful not t disturb you and Mrs. Harding."

"It wasn't you who disturbed me," said Thomas.

Fenny looked up.

"No, it was Sammy the cat."

"He frightened me, too, Mr. Harding," said Fenny seriously. "I thought it was you creeping about trying t catch me unawares like."

"I'd let him out," said Thomas.

"He's a big cat..."

"I was sure I'd let him out. I remembered."

"And he seemed bigger at night when everything wa quiet."

"Someone let him in," said Thomas incontrovertibly.

"That's right," said Fenny uneasily.

Thomas looked at him. "There's only one person with a key."

"Yes, Mr. Harding." Fenny agreed to this.

"Gladys," said Dora.

"That's right," said Fenny.

"We gave it to her so she shouldn't disturb us in the mornings."

"Ironic, isn't it?" said Thomas. He'd had a moment in the past, hadn't he, when he'd wondered if Gladys understood the meaning of the word.

Fenny was off on a different tack. "She didn't give me your food," he said hastily. "She wouldn't do a thing like that."

"No," said Thomas. Gladys wouldn't steal. They knew that. That's why they gave her the key. She might harbour a young man on the run, wanted for murder, might deceive the law, might use his house for someone else's shelter, but she would not steal. For a long moment Thomas's mind went back beyond the Barbarys to a man he hadn't given much thought to—Gerald Cloake. Gerald Cloake had done no worse than Gladys—giving shelter and comfort to a wanted man, fed him, used his own house—this same house—in which to do it. And he had gone to prison and been stripped of his possessions for his pains. There had been no murder there either—just the form of a religion. They said history repeated itself...

"Your mother," said Thomas, coming back to the present, "has been cooking for you, Fenny, hasn't she?"

"That's right, Mr. Harding."

Suddenly everything fell into place.

"She knew all the time."

"That's right, Mr. Harding. She didn't believe as how I'd have hurt my Mary." The faintest suspicion of a grin came over his face. "Otherwise I do believe as how she'd have handed me over herself."

"I think she would, too," agreed Thomas.

Tad was beginning to get restive but Thomas hadn't finished.

"Charlie Ford's got something to do with this, hasn't he?"

"Him and my Dad were mates," said Fenny, as if that explained everything.

"You couldn't have known to come here," said Thomas. "Not on your own."

"No," admitted Fenny. "It was his idea."

"He knew all about the hide," said Thomas slowly, "and he was the only person apart from me who knew how to open it."

"I didn't like it at first," said Fenny simply, "but it was that or prison, so I came here."

"Then," snorted Thomas, "having got you in here while our backs were turned Charlie Ford comes along and rigs up a couple of screws."

Fenny looked uneasily at Thomas.

"Two screws," repeated Thomas bitterly, "and a cock-and-bull story about some electricity wires."

"That's right, Mr. Harding. Charlie Ford—he found that floor board when he came to lay that wire through that you asked for."

"And he didn't tell me," said Thomas sadly.

"Beautiful job, it is," offered Fenny. "All sprung in. You'd never have guessed."

"No."

"I popped in there whenever I heard anyone talking about coming in."

"He would sure have been hearing a lot about the Barbarys," drawled Tad.

"Yes, I have," said Fenny sincerely. "It's sort of taken my mind off things a bit."

"Has it?" said Thomas drily.

"But it's made me certain sure about one thing, Mr Harding, and that's not to leave everything to justice. That boy you've been talking so much about . . ."

"Toby Barbary."

"Well, he didn't get justice, did he? Not in the end or at any other time."

"I suppose you could look at it that way."

"And this man that you think killed him, he got off didn't he? Even though all Easterbrook thought he'd done it."

"That was a hundred and fifty years ago," said Thomas. "Things have changed since then."

"Human nature hasn't," retorted Fenny, unanswerably. "Otherwise my Mary would still be alive, wouldn't she?"

Thomas sat down. This excitement was a bit much for him and he had just been visited by a new and disturbing thought.

"Fenny, let's forget the Barbarys and this hide for a moment—you're just trying to delay us, aren't you?"

The young man's face went blank. "Me, Mr. Harding?"

"Yes, Fenny, you." He was more certain than ever now. "There's something happening tonight, isn't there?"

"Tonight?" Fenny's voice went as blank as his face.

"Tonight," said Thomas briskly. "In the church, I should say, at a guess."

Tad bent over him solicitously. "How do you know that, Mr. Harding?"

"We saw them, Tad, remember? Going in. Gladys and Charlie Ford and Mrs. Fenny."

"So we did but—"

"When we were leaving the churchyard," said Thomas. "Ask Fenny here, I think you'll find he knows."

"That's right, Mr. Harding," said Fenny dully. "It was tonight."

"What was tonight?" asked Tad.

Thomas looked up shrewdly. "The reckoning, Fenny?"

"Yes, Mr. Harding, you could call it that."

"Will they be safe?"

"There's three to one, Mr. Harding."

"Two of them are women," said Thomas crisply, "and one of them an old woman at that. Tad, ring Inspector Bream and tell him."

Tad strode across the room. "Sure thing, Mr. Harding. It won't take him long to get here."

"Not here, boy. There's no use him coming here."

"But what about this guy Fenny?"

"He's all right," snapped Thomas. "It's his mother who's in danger and Gladys and Charlie Ford. Send him to the church and get my coat. We're going there, too. Come on, Fenny."

He waved his wife away and started for the door.

They were halfway to the church when they heard it; the long slow tolling of the funeral bell.

Thomas stopped. "Fenny, do you know what that means?"

"That it's all over, Mr. Harding." There was no excitement in his voice now. "They thought I would hear it at the Manor."

Suddenly Tad gave a shout. "I can see someone running... look."

Thomas spun round. "Where?"

"Over there. Down the path to the almshouses."

Thomas screwed up his eyes, but the running figure was already a blur.

They could see a knot of people moving about near the church now, too. Dim, indistinguishable forms in the late evening light. There was one, though, that was too distinctive for Thomas not to recognise.

It was the Rector.

At the other end of the churchyard a police car drew up and disgorged hurrying men. They spread out in all directions, one of them beginning to run down the churchyard path that led across the green to the almshouses and the river.

They drew level with the Rector. The Inspector came up to him urgently.

"You're too late," said the Rector.

Bream swung his torch round in a wide arc. "Which way did he go, sir?"

"That way..."

Bream shone the great beam down the path to the almshouses.

"You won't get him now," said Mr. Martindale slowly. "That path only leads one way."

"To...? Where does it lead, sir? This is important—we must know."

The Rector leaned wearily against the churchyard wall. "You will have him in the morning, Inspector. May God have mercy on his soul."

Bream stared sharply at the Rector. "I don't understand you, sir."

The Rector shook his head speechlessly.

Thomas spoke. "I think, Inspector, that Mr. Martindale means that you will find him—find his body—in the river. By morning it will be in the old mill dam down-stream." He hesitated, shades of the Barbarys flitting through his mind. "I think that's—"

Alan Fenny interrupted him in a harsh voice. "Bodies from Easterbrook always fetch up in the old mill dam, Inspector. Always have, always will."

There were suddenly lights everywhere in the church-yard and noises in all directions too.

They hastened towards the church, Thomas painfully conscious now of having done too much too quickly.

Charlie Ford was half sitting, half lying in a pew, Mrs. Fenny and Gladys tending a large and rapidly increasing lump on his forehead. They viewed the police without surprise.

Tad tugged at Thomas's sleeve. "Mr. Harding, who was it went to the river?"

Thomas sat down in the first pew he could find.

"Cousens, of course," he said. "Cyril Cousens, the organist. Didn't you know?"

Seventeen

"Living quietly in the country," said Dora. "That was wha
you were supposed to be doing."

Thomas opened an eye and shut it again quickly. Ther
was a very bright light coming from somewhere an
shining right in his face.

Dora hadn't sounded very far away. Perhaps if he shade
his eyes from the strong light he would be able to see he
He tried to bring his arm up to shade his eyes but ther
was something stopping him, weighting him down. . . .

"It's only the eiderdown," said Dora. She was standin
at the foot of his bed. He could see that much now, but th
bright light was still there, hurting his eyes.

If only they would take it away he would be able to se
again. He struggled on to his elbow and put up his othe
hand.

"It's the sun," he said.

"Yes," said Dora.

He sank back on to his pillow. A confused medley c
memory came flooding into his mind . . .

Of Mrs. Fenny waving a piece of paper in front of th
Inspector and croaking triumphantly: "A confession."

Of Alan Fenny, words tumbling out of him now as i
they would never stop. "He was always a bit sweet o
Mary, but she wouldn't have anything of him. That's wh
he turned nasty, I reckon."

Of Charlie Ford peering out from under the swellin
over his eye. "The poor girl paid him what she had an
then when he'd bled her white he asked for more."

"Breakfast," said Dora.

"I don't remember coming home."

"You fainted when you stood up," she said. "It took four of them to get you upstairs."

"Which four?" asked Thomas with interest.

"Tad, the doctor and two policemen."

"Fenny?"

"He went away with the Inspector but he didn't seem too worried about it."

"Charlie Ford?"

"Charlie Ford," said Dora with satisfaction, "has the biggest black-eye I have seen for a long time."

"He did what he could," said Thomas.

"In our house." She poured out some coffee for him. "Shall you be giving audiences this morning?"

"Audiences?"

"There are a number of people who want to see you. Toast?"

"Thank you," weakly. "Which people?"

"Tad, for a start. I've had difficulty in keeping him out. And Inspector Bream. Oh, and Gladys."

"Gladys?"

"Gladys has something she wishes to say to you."

In the end she brought the Inspector in first. He refused a chair and stood awkwardly at the foot of the bed. He declined coffee, too.

"I thought you ought to be told, Mr. Harding, that a body, believed to be that of Cyril Cousens, was removed from the mill dam just after daylight this morning."

"Thank you," said Thomas gravely.

"And that, as far as we can see, a certain signed statement purporting to have been written by the said Cyril Cousens in the presence of..."

Thomas stirred his coffee vigorously.

Bream tried again. "Written in the presence of several witnesses..."

Thomas nodded.

"...Absolves the man Fenny from having any part in his wife's death. He will no doubt be released from custody during this morning."

"It was blackmail then?"

"We are acting on that assumption," said the policeman cautiously. "It seems that Mary Fenny did have a secret.

We think that she told the Rector about it one day in the church."

"Confession," said Thomas.

"Very likely." He coughed. "It seems probable that Cyril Cousens was in the organ loft and heard what she had to say. Simple, isn't it?"

"Horribly simple." Thomas struggled into a sitting position. "There's just one thing I would like to know. That signed confession that Mrs. Fenny was waving about—how did they get it?"

"One man and two women?" The Inspector's back was to the sunlight so Thomas couldn't see his face. "I don't know officially, sir, and I don't want to be told."

"Quite . . ."

"This church of yours has got a new organ, hasn't it?"

"It has."

"The very latest thing in electric organs, you might say?"

"You might," said Thomas fervently. "As it happens I helped pay for it."

"And do you happen to know who installed it?"

"Charlie Ford, I expect," said Thomas promptly. "He does most of the electrical work round here . . ." He stopped. Was it his imagination or was Bream grinning?

"Wired up very nicely, it was," said Bream reminiscently, "when we got there."

"You mean," said Thomas, comprehension dawning, "that Ford had . . ."

Bream nodded. "I don't know how he did it, but I think they must have waited until Cousens had sat down at the organ to play and then thrown some sort of switch."

"Well I never," said Thomas. "A man of parts, our Charlie Ford."

"You might say," said Bream, staring at the ceiling, "quite unofficially of course—that they'd rigged up their own electric chair. Cousens must have got a shock every time he moved."

"But he hit Charlie Ford."

"That, sir, was afterwards. They traded his confession

r a getaway—and, I gather, for not electrocuting him on
e spot."

"Did they indeed?"

"Highly improper, of course."

"Of course."

"He was on his way when he saw us in the churchyard
d realised the game was up."

"The Rector," said Thomas. "What was he doing there?"

"He heard the church bell and came to see what was
·ing on."

"That was a message," said Thomas. "Meant to tell Alan
·nny in his hide here that all was well."

"Yes, sir, we gathered that." He turned to go. "Had us
·th fixed, sir, didn't he, in that hole?"

The next knock on the door produced Gladys.

"Excuse me, Mr. Harding, but are you finished with
·at tray?"

"Yes, thank you, Gladys."

"Mr. Harding..." She picked up the tray and stood by
·e bed. "We hope you didn't mind about Alan being in
·ur hole."

"Not at all," said Thomas politely. "After all, you
·dn't—er—know of a better one, did you?"

"No," said Gladys frankly, "we didn't."

"That's all right then, isn't it?"

She paused, the tray balanced against her hip. "Charlie
·rd says he'll be round first thing..."

"What for?"

"That plug, Mr. Harding, that you wanted by the fire-
·ace. You hadn't forgotten, had you?"

"I had rather," admitted Thomas. "Something put it out
·my mind."

It was half past twelve before Thomas dressed and went
·wnstairs. He found Tad in the drawing-room
·ntemplating the empty hide.

"Beautiful job of work Nicholas Owen made of it," said
·d.

"Craftsmen were craftsmen then," said Thomas
·sently, beginning to go through his post.

Dora came in with three glasses of sherry on a tray. "I
·el we've earned this."

"There's not a lot of the Fenny mystery left," admitte Thomas, "and I doubt if we can go any further with th Barbary one." He turned over a brown paper parcel in a abstracted manner.

"Too soon to give up yet," said Tad robustly. "I've on been at it for five days—that is, if you can put up with n a bit longer."

"Five days!" echoed Dora.

"It seems weeks," declared Thomas with feeling. "Is only five days?"

"That's all." Tad smiled slightly. "Could you bear it for few more?"

"My dear boy," protested Dora, "we enjoy having you

"I do believe she's done it," whispered Thoma unfolding layers of brown paper in a reverent fashion.

"Who?" asked Dora.

"Miss Porteous. The admirable Miss Porteous, the be secretary a man could have—she's done it."

"Done what?"

Thomas lifted his face to them both. "She's found a cop of the Barbary family history."

Tad was at his side in a flash, grinning all over his fac "Attagirl! or do you say 'Bully for Miss Porteous'?"

"Is it the right one?" Dora wanted to know.

"Miss Porteous," said Thomas confidently, "never mad a mistake in her life." He opened the cover and read alou "'Printed for Sir Toby Barbary of Easterbrook by Pet Billings, Printer, at his Press in Ox Lane, Callefor 1812'."

"The missing pages," breathed Dora. "Are they there

Thomas leafed carefully through the short history of th Cloake family.

"They were near the front," said Dora excitedly, "in th bit about the house before he started on the family part

They all watched as Thomas turned over page after pag in the right order.

"It was after it mentioned 'secret worship' on a left-han page," said Dora, looking over his shoulder, and then moment later she put out a hand. "There, there..."

Thomas stopped. On the left-hand page was the famili paragraph.

All three pairs of eyes turned as one to the right-hand page, the page that had been missing in the volume in the Halleford Public Library.

Thomas took a deep breath and began to read aloud. "The Manor was a well-known Catholic one, ideal for the purpose of secret worship on account of its secluded position in a small village. I have been unable to find who built it but the handiwork of Nicholas,' here's where the next page begins, 'Owen'! Nicholas Owen! That man Mellon was right after all."

"Oh, do go on, Thomas. What does it say next?"

" 'The handiwork of Nicholas Owen can be seen in the construction of a priest's hide and chapel.' "

"And chapel!" repeated Tad.

"Mellon was right again, then," exclaimed Thomas. "He said all along there would have been a chapel too. We looked everywhere for it, didn't we, Dora?"

"You did," agreed his wife drily, "and ended up in bed with the effort."

"Without finding it," said Tad.

"Without finding even the faintest whiff of incense. And Mellon kept on saying that the priest would have had somewhere to say Mass." He chuckled delightedly. "He was right after all. I wonder where it is?"

"You could read on," suggested Dora.

Thomas grinned. He never confused his wife's habitual understatement with sarcasm.

" 'The former','" he read aloud, " 'is behind the panelling to the left-hand of the chimney in the drawing-room. It is revealed by the pressing of part of the fourth panel from the right in a certain manner that I learnt from my father. Inside, is space enough for a man to be comfortable for a week.' "

"We know all that," said Dora impatiently. "What about the chapel?"

" 'The chapel','" went on Thomas slowly, " 'is near by in the roof of another place and is as secret as the hiding place. To enter it a man must swing his whole weight on the second beam and stoop very low. It is bigger than the other and reckoned a very clever piece of work.' "

"But where is it?" demanded Tad insistently.

"'Priests could come and go between the Manor and this place.'"

"What place?" cried Tad.

"'Secretly and be sure they could hide from the pursui vants in either building. They were Jesuits lately lande from the continent by sea and given shelter by th Cloakes.'"

"Poor things," said Dora spontaneously.

"Until 1587," said Thomas. "There was no more shelte after that."

"But where?..." began Tad again.

"Yew Tree Cottage, of course." Thomas shut the boo thoughtfully. "We ought to have guessed. I was wron about that being a smugglers' road and so was Mrs Meredith."

"Who was Mrs. Meredith?"

"She lived here before the war. She thought it was smugglers' road too. It wasn't. It's much earlier than that It's a sunken road just to connect the Manor with Yew Tre Cottage and the village."

"So that..."

But Thomas went on following his own train of thought "And the priest would live here and then go down there t say Mass. You would have to be pretty close to see anyon walking that road."

"What a discovery!" burst out Tad, refusing to kee quiet any longer. "A hidden chapel as well as a priest hide."

"And the Barbarys didn't know about the bolt-hole i the hide, after all, did they?" said Dora. "Or Sir Tob would have mentioned it here."

"Just as well he didn't," said Thomas, "or we woul never have found the skeleton in the first place." He rose "I'll ring Mellon straightaway and that Miss—what's he name?"

"Casterton."

But Tad and Thomas couldn't bring themselves to wai for the historian to arrive, and as soon after luncheon a they decently could they were knocking on the door o Yew Tree Cottage.

"I'm sure you must be mistaken," said Miss Casterton

"but you're very welcome to look. Do take your time going up—it's such a narrow, steep stairway that I seldom use it myself. There's only the one little room up there anyway."

Thomas saved his breath for the stairs. They were steep and dark and inconvenient, just as she had said, but eventually the three of them got to the top.

"He said the second beam," panted Thomas, "but he didn't say second to what."

"There's no shortage of beams anyway," said Tad. Even he was a little out of breath. "We're practically in the rafters."

He stood alertly in the middle of the room.

"If we were to take the second one from the top of the stairs," began Thomas, "which would be . . ."

"Look over there," said Tad. "At the second one from the horizontal."

"That's the tie beam. What about it?"

"The second one from that's not quite touching at the top."

Thomas moved up to it. "It's not taking any weight at all, is it? What did the book say?"

Tad came alongside him. "'A man must swing his whole weight on the beam and stoop low.'"

In the end it needed their combined weights to shift the beam on its ancient pivot and then the bottom half swung out and they were staring into a dark space.

Thomas switched on the torch and poked it forward.

"Sir Toby was right about stooping low," said Tad. "I can just crawl in from where I am now."

"Go ahead," instructed Thomas.

Tad screwed his head round and looked at him.

"Of course," said Thomas. "Go in and see how your ancestors left it."

Tad grinned and disappeared.

"Come in," he called back a moment later. "There's plenty of room once you're inside."

Thomas squeezed through the low, narrow entry.

"There's no window," said Tad, "but we're right up in the roof and there's a fair bit of light between the shingles. They'd have had candles, I suppose."

Thomas nodded.

"Pretty clever idea to have the chapel away from the house," went on Tad. "The Manor's the place those priest hunters would have searched first. It would give the congregation time to get away."

"And people—poor people—could have come here less conspicuously than to the Manor."

Tad swung his torch round. "Looks like one of the ladies left her bag behind." He stooped to the floor and picked up a little embroidered bag, dusty but intact. "Kind of touching, isn't it?"

Thomas looked at the delicate work and nodded. "I think this chapel is why Giles Shambrook wanted this cottage."

"How come?" said Tad, still swinging the torch round.

"If," said Thomas slowly, "he owned Yew Tree Cottage and could demonstrate to all and sundry that there was a chapel here then he would have been much more likely to have been listened to if he had decided to tell the world about Toby Barbary and the secret hide."

Tad wasn't listening. He had stopped swinging the torch and was holding it steady now.

"Take a look at that, will you, Mr. Harding?" he said in a strange voice. "Do you see what I see?"

Thomas followed his gaze.

Lying in the dust on the floor was one old shoe.

"I guess," said Tad with difficulty, "that this is what you call the pay-off."

"Giles Shambrook's hold over Sir Richard," said Thomas, "that's what it was."

They went silently out of the little room in the rafters, Tad still holding in his hand the little embroidered bag.

Miss Casterton was there waiting for them.

"What did you find?" she asked uncertainly.

"An old shoe," said Tad quietly, "and this little bag. We know about the shoe, but this belonged to some lady who forgot it."

"No," said Miss Casterton.

Tad looked up. "No?"

She shook her head. "That's a pyx-bag you've got there. I've seen them before."

"A pyx-bag?"

She nodded briskly. "You know. For consecrated bread."

"No," said Tad. "I didn't know." He turned to Thomas, and said awkwardly: "Mr. Harding, I still have a duty to perform to the owner of that shoe."

Thomas nodded. "I hadn't forgotten."

"After all," said Tad, "I am Toby Barbary's only living relative."

Eighteen

It was Saturday morning, just eight days since Tad arrived in Easterbrook.

Thomas and Dora were standing in the Barbary pew in the church. The bell was being tolled and the morning sun was filtering through a dozen stained glass windows.

They were not alone.

A few moments earlier Mrs. Fenny had walked in and now stood surveying the scene with her customary aplomb. A dapper Archibald Mellon was there, his attention straying to the fabric of the church. He had been followed in to the church by two maiden ladies, upright and staid, strangers to Thomas. They made their way majestically to a pew while Dora bent her head towards him and whispered, "The Misses Siskin. You remember."

Miss Casterton came in behind them, smiling in their direction.

Thomas nodded back and lifted his eyes just in time to catch half a grin from the doctor. Inspector Bream came in with Constable Wilkins and Thomas reflected that the police had a very nice sense of the fitness of things.

Then the church door opened again.

"I do believe..." murmured Dora. "No, it can't be..."

Thomas screwed his head round. "What can't be?"

"It is," said Dora.

An extraordinary sight met his eyes. An incredibly bent old lady, dressed in black, and sitting in an invalid chair, was being wheeled into the church.

"Gladys's mother," agreed Thomas.

Gladys settled her mother in a side aisle and sat down.

Then the choir made their way slowly up the nave, boys first and then the men. Thomas turned his head slightly as they went by. Alan Fenny was there, clean-shaven now, but still hollow-cheeked and white. There was a stranger at the organ.

The tolling of the bell stopped and they could hear the voice of the Rector.

Charlie Ford, eye still a little black, superintended the setting of the oaken coffin he had made for Toby Barbary on to the waiting trestles. A solitary wreath of roses lay on it.

Sir Thaddeus Barbary of Easterbrook, fifteenth of that name, stepped from behind the coffin and stood at Thomas's side in the Barbary pew.

Together they looked up at the immutable memorials to Colonel Sir Toby Barbary, 8th Baronet, Colonel of the 123rd, The Calleshire Regiment, Justice of the Peace, and to Sir Richard Barbary, 9th Baronet, Benefactor of this Parish.

ABOUT THE AUTHOR

CATHERINE AIRD had never tried her hand at writing suspense stories before publishing *The Religious Body*—a novel which immediately established her as one of the genre's most talented writers. *A Late Phoenix, The Stately Home Murder, His Burial Too, Some Die Eloquent, Henrietta Who?* and *A Most Contagious Game* have subsequently enhanced her reputation. Her ancestry is Scottish, but she now lives in a village in East Kent, near Canterbury, where she serves as an aid to her father, a doctor, and takes an interest in local affairs.

For 15 years, Catherine Aird's mysteries have won praises for their brilliant plotting and style. Established alongside other successful English mystery ladies, she continues to thrill old and new mystery fans alike.

CIRCLE OF LOVE

Step out of your world and enter the Circle of Love.